A KISS FOR SOLSTICE

MIDNIGHT SUN SUPERNATURALS BOOK ONE

ELIZABETH ALLYN-DEAN

 Created with Vellum

Thank you to the friends and family who have supported me through this story's journey. In particular, I want to thank my son Alex, who inspired the fighter's spirit of the hero of this story through his love for all things mixed martial arts and his insistence I love it too (and for not minding my laughing whenever he says, "rear naked choke"). A special thanks to Gwen Knight, Jori Buchanan, and Neva Post for their unwavering encouragement, not to mention reading and rereading this story until they knew it almost as well as me.

Cover design by Covermint

Her kiss brought him back from the dead...

Dax Rand has a knack for finding trouble, and this time he's won the grand prize—eternity in an unmarked shallow grave. When an angel brings him back from death with her magical kiss, he's sure his luck is finally changing for the better. But would an angel make him feel such sinful things?

Zelda Melik is no angel. Just a magnet for the dead, which makes her a valuable asset to her coven's power-hungry high priestess. But taking Zelda's sister hostage to ensure her obedience is going too far. Zelda needs help, and the Fates deliver in the form of a mostly dead, and incredibly hot, werewolf with a talent for kicking ass.

To win their freedom, Zelda is willing to do anything. Even bring a werewolf to a witch fight.

CHAPTER 1

"I think you've found us a new Solstice tradition." Lucy's shout vibrated in Zelda's ear, barely audible in the brouhaha. "This is perfect!"

"Yeah, nothing says 'holidays' like a hundred or so testosterone-poisoned guys egging on suped-up muscle heads determined to beat each other bloody," Zelda snarked.

Not that Lucy heard her. She'd succumbed to the masses, joining the raucous cheering. Like them, her attention was on the spotlighted, chain-link-enclosed platform at the center of the cavernous warehouse.

Two men—one who looked like a hairless silverback gorilla and the other who looked like a slightly less hairy Sasquatch—clashed inside the cage. Given that the fighters who participated in the monthly underground event were generally supernaturals, these 'men' were likely what they resembled. Everyone knew that Isadora Kane—CEO of Mabon Enterprises, the unofficial sponsor of the event, and High Priestess of Sleeping Lady Coven—had a knack for setting up entertaining matches.

Like two bull moose in rut, the men pitted their strength and aggression against one another. The squatter man roared, dropping his stance and charging, beefy arms coiling around the taller man's hips. Knocked off balance, he slammed against the chain-link, sweat and blood splattering everyone within twenty feet.

As Zelda wiped a sleeve across her face, she made a mental note. If she ever attended another fight night— and that was an enormous 'if'—she'd grab seats farther from the splash zone.

The posts flexed as the men pressed against the fencing, one throwing elbows and knees as the other curled to protect his head and ribs. By the time the bell signaled the end of the round, the crowd had reached a fevered pitch. As if the jarring sound had flipped an off switch, the men peeled apart and the crowd quieted, many retaking their seats.

Zelda leaned toward Lucy, taking the opportunity to give her coven sister a response she could hear. "Sure, perfect holiday entertainment."

"Hey, you invited me, remember?" Lucy wrapped an arm around Zelda's shoulders. Pulling her in tight, the witch winked. "You've got to admit, it's less vicious than coven gatherings. Definitely sweatier and bloodier though. At least here we get eye candy—buff dudes in their undies fighting to see who's top—"

The bell and resumed cheers cut off what Lucy might have said. But she'd made her point, one Zelda couldn't unhear. There *was* something about the men's grunting and grappling, an alpha male intensity that called to something primitive in her hindbrain and made her heart pound. It was primal, physical almost to the point of being sexual. Or maybe it had just been too long since she'd done any X-rated wrestling of her own.

The man standing behind Zelda and Lucy jostled against them, shouting, "Check out that rear naked choke. That dude's good." The scent of body spray was strong with this one, overpowering the fog of popcorn and beer smells inside the warehouse. A wide, white smile flashed against his dark skin in the dim lighting outside the ring. "Lock him in, Black!"

"See?" Lucy leaned in, lips nearly brushing Zelda's ear. "With names like that for their moves—not to mention all that hot, glistening man meat—it's like a live sex show."

"Watched in the company of a hundred other people," Zelda shot back with an exaggerated roll of her eyes. "At the first sign of genitals, I'm leaving."

"Seriously? Did you just say 'genitals'? You sound like a dried-up sex ed teacher." Lucy stuck her tongue out at Zelda as the crowd erupted into cheers.

It seemed the porny-sounding move had finished the match. The taller man sprawled on the mat as the squatter man prowled the periphery of the cage, pounding his fists against his chest in victory. As the referee declared the winner, two other men entered the ring and loaded the loser onto a bloodstained stretcher.

Zelda scanned the crowd as the cage emptied. When she spotted her reason for being at the fights—Isadora Kane—every muscle in her body coiled and her hands balled into fists. What she wouldn't give to get the woman into the ring for a couple rounds. She might not know anything about fighting with her fists or feet, but Zelda was sure that years of bottled up hatred for Isadora would erupt in a beat-down of legendary proportions.

High Priestess Isadora was holding court from a raised set of chairs near the mouth of the cage. Her goons —Russian werewolf brothers—flanked her like grim bookends, dwarfing everyone around them. But this was Isadora's show, and it was clear from her haughty expression and the regal wave of her hand that she knew it.

All the fighters belonged to Isadora in one way or another. Signing a contract with her was worse than making a deal with the Devil. She owned you, body and soul. Sure, when you were in her good graces, life was paradise. But when you were on her bad side—like Zelda and her sister Larissa—life was like the seventh circle of Hell.

Lucy's sharp elbow shattered Zelda's thoughts. "You might not be hoping for a wardrobe malfunction, but I am. Check out the hottie in the black and red trunks. Yum!" Lucy raked pink-nailed fingers through her blonde hair and dragged her tongue across an equally pink lower lip. "Damn! Why can't he be wearing tiny fight shorts like those last two?"

Despite herself, Zelda swung her gaze toward the new fighters entering the cage. She could say one thing about Lucy—the woman had good taste. Assuming one liked the tall, muscular, and tattooed type. Something fluttered deep in her belly as she sent her eyes traveling over the plates of muscle that made up the man's torso.

Nope, not my type at all.

Lucy's laughter jingled above the restless crowd's mutterings. "I better find something to wipe up the drool."

"Yeah, sure. You do that." Zelda tried to cover the flushing of her cheeks with a nonchalant tone and wave of her hand toward the concessions table. "Can you get me a drink while you're at it?"

When Lucy only laughed, sitting back in her chair, Zelda huffed in annoyance. "I wasn't kidding. I could really use a good, stiff drink."

"You could use a good, stiff something," Lucy teased. "And you're not alone."

Try as she might, Zelda couldn't tear her gaze from the dark-haired fighter. Sure, he reached male-model levels of hotness, but it was the way he moved that held her attention. Fluid, predatory grace. It was like watching a hungry tiger at the zoo, pacing the length of the enclosure, his focus on the slab of meat dangled in front of him.

Zelda's heart thudded as she imagined that intense gaze on her. She leaned toward the cage, curling her fingers around the back of the empty folding chair in front of her. Who was he?

She'd never seen him before, so he wasn't a member of Anchorage's Bold Peak Pack. Was he from one of the other Alaskan packs? One outside Alaska? Was he even a supernatural? Isadora liked to toss the occasional human in the ring, a chew toy for the younger, less experienced werewolves.

Zelda recognized the other fighter as one of Isadora's playthings, new to Bold Peak Pack. The werewolf, who went by the name Hunter, wasn't hard on the eyes either. Her coven sisters had given him an enthusiastic welcome, showing their appreciation in one way or another—completely on the down-low, of course. Isadora didn't like her witches petting her pups or offering them treats.

Hunter bounced from foot to foot and shook out his arms, then threw a few air punches. As the crowd chanted his name, he jogged a lap along the chain-link fencing, pumping his arms to encourage them to up their volume. They ate it up, roaring when he showboated with a backflip in the middle of the cage.

But the mystery fighter's expression never changed, his focus unshaken. His pacing continued, steady and purposeful, until the referee gestured him toward the cage's center.

"Yeah! Get him, Dax!" the man behind them cheered. He leaned in close to Lucy and Zelda, proclaiming, "That's my boy!"

"Which one?" Lucy's tone sparked with interest, not that the chatty guy needed any encouragement.

"Black and red trunks," the man answered, pride clear in his voice. Now he also had Zelda's attention. While she kept her eyes glued to the ring, she strained to hear what he had to say. "He's the biggest underdog of the night, but my money's on him to win before the first round's over."

"What's his name?" Lucy asked, the longing tone in

the question pulling Zelda's stare from the ring. She shot the woman a warning look, not that Lucy noticed. If Zelda didn't stop her, she'd be convincing this guy that he and his 'boy' should join them for drinks after the fight.

"Dax Rand. And I'm Jamie. We're brothers *and* training partners. What are your names?"

Brother? Zelda bounced her gaze between their new friend and the fighter in the ring. She and Lucy looked more like siblings than the two men. Of course, they could be pack mates—not that she sensed anything supernatural about Jamie. But then he was wearing enough body spray to cover the telltale stench of wolf.

Lucy flicked blonde hair over her shoulder before presenting her hand to Jamie. "I'm Lucy, and this is Zelda. So, you're a fighter too? And brothers? Interesting."

Zelda couldn't stop from rolling her eyes as Lucy chatted the guy up, her switch now firmly flipped to flirt mode. Bringing her coven sister to a place like this was dangerous, like setting a kid loose in a toy store. Any shiny new toy she brought home would be forgotten and left on the floor for Zelda to trip over in the morning.

When the bell sounded, signaling the start of the fight, a hush fell over the crowd. The men circled inside the cage, testing each other with cautious jabs and kicks. But the crowd exploded into raucous cheers when Dax suddenly pounced, fists swinging for Hunter's head and feet battering his legs. The attack was sudden, ferocious, and over in less than twenty seconds.

When Hunter dropped to the mat, curling into a ball, Dax followed him, fists and elbows slamming into his opponent's head. After a few seconds of pummeling the guy, he stopped. Leaping to his feet, he stalked to the far side of the cage, pacing as the referee moved in to check the unmoving man.

The official shook his head, signaling for someone to retrieve the downed fighter, then strode toward Dax. Gripping the man's wrist, he raised the gloved hand in victory.

The crowd went wild, including Lucy and Jamie, jumping up and down while chanting Dax's name. But he stayed oddly reserved, acknowledging the crowd with an indifferent wave of his hand as he left the cage. Was he angry that the fight was over so fast? He didn't even stop to talk to any of the people clapping him on the shoulder in congratulations as he passed, just offered a curt nod.

When High Priestess Isadora rose and stepped forward to congratulate him, and he strode past as if he didn't see her, Zelda couldn't resist joining the cheering. The look on the woman's face was priceless—confusion, shock, and then anger. Zelda could practically hear the woman's thoughts: *No one ignores Queen Isadora!* For a second, it seemed she was going to send her goons after him, and they certainly looked game, but she only sent a dismissive wave toward Dax's back and flounced onto her chair.

Goddess, I need to meet this man. A giddy sort of nervousness rushed through Zelda at the thought. She'd never seen someone blow off Isadora like that, other than her father. *So, is he powerful, reckless, or just stupid?*

"See, I told you!" Jamie's large hands thudded the

women's backs, his excitement enough to nearly knock them from their feet. "My bro just won me enough to pay rent on our pad *and* our gym dues for the next couple months."

Lucy wrapped an arm around Zelda, wagging her eyebrows. "Exciting, right?" For as long as Zelda had known Lucy, she'd had an appetite for hot guys, but the mention of money made her insatiable.

"Yeah, exciting." Zelda turned her eyes back toward the area used as a locker room, willing Dax to reemerge.

More like intriguing. Her thoughts spun. The guy was a brutal fighter, but more importantly, he wasn't one of Isadora's pets. And if he was participating in an underground fighting ring, he was likely a bit morally flexible, motivated by something other than personal safety. Most werewolves she'd met were—it came with the lifestyle—but once they chose their loyalties, they fought to the death to protect them. Zelda could use someone like that on her side, someone who would help rescue Larissa for the right incentive.

"So, what do you think?" Lucy gave Zelda a nudge, jolting her from her thoughts.

I think he's exactly what I need. "About?"

"Goddess, what is wrong with you tonight? You're so distracted." Lucy gave a teasing pout, one that she usually aimed at guys to get what she wanted. "Jamie said he and Dax are probably going out after this to celebrate, that he'd love for us to hang out with them."

Zelda glared in Isadora's direction, the scowl twisting the muscles in her face into knots, ones that multiplied and spread through her body. She'd planned to follow the high priestess after the fights, hoping the woman would lead her to whatever evil secret lair she'd stashed Larissa in.

No more groveling for promises that Isadora always broke. No more doing whatever Isadora demanded as payment for the smallest sign that her sister was all right. Zelda would free Larissa and escape Anchorage by New Year's, or she'd die trying.

"I thought we were—"

"Oh, come on, Zelda. Like Isadora is going anywhere but Coven House after she leaves here. She needs to lead the Solstice feast and ritual." Lucy released Zelda, her gaze dropping to the ground. "Look, Larissa will be fine for one more night. Maybe Isadora will even bring her to Coven House tonight. She promised she would after the last job you pulled for her, right? I know I told you I'd help, but if we try to rescue her and screw up, Isadora will hurt us, Larissa, maybe the whole coven."

As much as Zelda hated to admit it, Lucy was right. If she enlisted her coven sisters' help in freeing Larissa, Isadora would have an excuse to punish them all. She needed to keep them out of it.

But if her last failed rescue attempt had taught her anything, it was that she couldn't do it alone. She needed help beyond her familiars or spirit allies. Her thoughts returned once again to the fighter, Dax. It couldn't hurt to explore her options, right? She'd just have to be careful about it.

"Fine, you win. New plan. Drinks with Jamie and his brother before heading back to Coven House."

A smile lit Lucy's face, not directed at Zelda but over

her shoulder. She turned to look, her pulse quickening when she realized Dax was heading toward them. She smoothed hasty hands over her hair, blouse, and jeans. The self-grooming served a dual purpose, the cloth wicking away the sudden clamminess of her palms.

Jamie pushed past, vaulting over the chairs in front of them. A smile tugged at the corners of Dax's mouth as his brother rushed toward him, grabbing him in a back-pounding, rib-crushing hug. He seemed fairly calm for a guy who'd just won a fight, his excitement nowhere near his brother's.

"Goddess, he's even hotter than I thought," Lucy sighed dreamily. "I've got him, and you can have Jamie. Thank you for agreeing to go along with this. If it works out, I owe you one."

Zelda tried to look cool and collected as the men approached, answering Lucy with a noncommittal shrug. Jamie was a fine enough male specimen, but Dax was the one she was interested in. Strictly for business purposes, of course.

"Dax, this is Lucy and Zelda. I invited them to come with us to The Farm."

As Dax's dark eyes swept over them, Zelda could sympathize with Lucy's squirming. No man who regularly took punches to the face should have such fabulous bone structure. The slight bump on the bridge of his nose, where it had likely been broken, and the two scars—one cutting through a dark eyebrow and another below his full lower lip—gave his face character. A clear bad boy appeal. Not that she went for that kind of thing.

Yeah, right.

She shook the thoughts from her head. She didn't need him for his looks, just his fists. Her gaze dropped to his hands. Just moments before, he'd used them to pummel another living being into unconsciousness and walked away like it was nothing. They should look dangerous, but they just looked strong, capable.

Just like his muscular, tattooed arms. At this distance, she could see the tattoos were high quality—one colorful Japanese-style sleeve featuring something scaled and a tiger, the other sleeve an eclectic collection of black and gray art. Did they represent something for him? Tell the story of his life? She didn't ponder that for too long, distracted by his broad shoulders and solid chest, showcased in a tight red T-shirt with the logo from an Anchorage gym. A local?

Well, he looks very—her mind stuttered over possible descriptors—*sturdy, muscular... appealing.* Heat started in her cheeks and spread downward as her fingers twitched with the desire to brush over the ridged muscles visible through the light cotton of his T-shirt.

She found herself leaning in, breathing deep. No telltale tang of wolf. And she didn't feel the shiver of magic coming from him. Could he be human? If so, how did he beat a werewolf? Admittedly, his opponent was cocky and new to his fangs and the pack, but such a win was as unlikely as Zelda out-magicking Isadora.

Now she really was intrigued.

"Not tonight. I'm not in the mood to party." Dax's tone was as dismissive as his gaze. "You need a lift home, Jamie, or are you going with them?"

"You sure, bro?" Jamie asked.

Dax didn't say another word, only eyeballing Jamie for a heartbeat or two before walking away.

"Sorry." Jamie turned back to the women with an apologetic grin. "It was nice meeting you. Maybe I'll see you around, like at the next fight night."

"You too." Lucy waved as he trotted after his brother. She turned back to Zelda, her friendly smile melting into open-mouthed surprise. "He thought we were groupies. And totally blew us off. When has that ever happened?"

"I don't know about you, but I've never had anyone look at me like that."

"Like what?"

"Like I was a *Girls Gone Wild* bimbo." Zelda wasn't sure if she was annoyed or amused. She'd spent her life learning to be mostly invisible. Coming from a long line of powerful witches—not to mention being a magnet for the dead—tended to leave a taint that made most people uncomfortable. It was better to be the weird, easily dismissed wallflower than the potentially dangerous and powerful heir to the Melik dynasty.

"Oh, I get that look all the time. But I've never had a guy blow me off like that." The frown that creased Lucy's brow was uncharacteristic. The pretty, perky, sorority-girl wannabe generally avoided any facial expressions that might cause wrinkles. "You're bad luck. Remind me never to let you play wingwoman again."

Zelda sighed, muttering, "You've no idea."

Bad luck seemed to follow Zelda, a dark cloud that enveloped those she let too close. For the last five years, that cloud had gone by the name of Isadora Kane. The woman had taken, or chased away, everyone Zelda cared about—coven sisters, her blood sister, her father, potential boyfriends. Isadora turned them all into bargaining chips.

Lucy's eyes widened and swung to a spot beyond Zelda's shoulder. When Zelda turned to look, she face-planted into a man's chest. Well, not a man, a werewolf. There was no doubting the sharp, musky smell that battered her nose.

A glance upward confirmed her fear. Dimitri. Of Isadora's wolves, he was the worst. The alpha of the Bold Peak Pack always looked at the witches in Coven House like they were little piggies he wanted to devour. Isadora must have realized Zelda was at the fights and sent her mutt to play fetch.

Dimitri's hand darted out and caught Zelda's arm when she tried to take a step back. "Your mother—"

"She's not my mother." Zelda yelped when the werewolf's grip tightened, sending a painful ping zipping from her upper arm to her fingertips, removing all feeling in its wake. "Let me go," *you stinking wolf.* Somehow, she managed to keep from saying that last bit aloud.

She might have been braver if she hadn't felt Lucy abandon her back. Not that she blamed her coven sister for fleeing. In fact, she was glad for it. Zelda had been selfish and reckless to bring the woman to the fights and put her in possible danger. The last thing she wanted was to hand Isadora another hostage.

"Come. Now." He practically picked Zelda up as he turned.

"I bet the ladies love—" Her attempt at smartassery ended in a yelp when the werewolf's fingers bit deeper into the muscle of her arm.

The crowd parted as Dimitri stalked back toward Isadora. Zelda stumbled as she tried to keep up with his long stride. She scanned the crowd, looking for any hint of help. Nothing. The minute her eyes met anyone's, they looked away. None that knew Isadora Kane, or her goons, dared cross her. Even Zelda's father had abandoned the coven and fled the country rather than deal with her.

Isadora's cold emerald stare locked onto Zelda, a smile pulling at red-lacquered lips when Dimitri presented her like a dog showing his master his favorite bone.

"Ah, my dear Grizelda. Delightful to see you. Thank you for saving me the trouble of tracking you down before tonight's ritual. I need your services." Isadora's saccharine tone and equally fake smile sent a chill up Zelda's spine.

"I can't—"

"How many times must we go over this, child? Your refusal has consequences. Although I'm sure my associate"—she gestured to the werewolf looming behind Zelda, her expression magnanimous—"would thank you for it. I do believe he enjoys his job more than is appropriate. But then your sister is such a pretty girl."

Fury flared in Zelda's belly. "Don't you dare turn that beast on her." Dimitri's tightening grip and warning growl forced the flame down to a simmer. "I've done everything you've asked."

"If you continue to do so, she'll remain safe and well cared for." Isadora fingered the thick silver cuff at her wrist, the spelled metal a sign of her status as high priestess. "Now, will you do as I ask?"

"As if I have a choice."

"You've always had a choice, dear. But I'll take that as an agreement." Blood-red nails flashed dangerously, a marked contrast to the casual wave of her hand. "There's a meeting tonight between some very important people, and I need a fly on the wall. Or should I say a spirit's ears in the room. That's within your power, yes?"

"Just to listen and report? Nothing else?"

"For the moment." Isadora sat back in her chair, pulling her phone from her purse. "Dimitri will take you where you need to go and provide the necessary details. Once you're done, I expect to see you at the feast. Do what I ask, and do it well, and maybe your sister will be able to join us at Coven House tonight."

Despite herself, Zelda's heart swelled at the thought. It had been a month since she'd last seen Larissa. "I thought my last job—"

"That was before you angered me by plotting with your coven sister tonight. But bring me what I want this time, and I'll forgive your transgression and perhaps even reward your success." As Dimitri's grip tightened around her arms again and he turned her to leave, Isadora's voice chimed at her back. "You know, Grizelda, you'd be so much prettier if you'd smile. You're far too serious."

"I'll smile when you're finally out of our lives," Zelda muttered. It was probably for the best that the words were lost to the crowd's renewed cheering.

CHAPTER 2

A WOMAN'S PLEAS AND A MAN'S LOW, ANGRY RUMBLE slipped past the heavy wooden door to burrow into Dax's ears. Despite not being able to understand what they were saying—it sounded like they were speaking Russian—it was disturbingly familiar. For a moment, he was a twelve-year-old with his ear pressed to the roughly patched drywall between his and his sister Jennie's bedroom. Just like then, his teeth and fists clenched so tightly that their creaking nearly drowned out all other sounds. Unlike then, his brother Jamie wasn't there to keep him from doing something stupid.

Heavy footsteps on the other side of Mabon Enterprises' door chased Dax into the empty office across the hall. He watched from the shadows as a man stalked through the opening. Unlike the plodding, drunken stumbling of Dax's former foster father, this man moved like a fighter, all swagger. Tall and heavily muscled, he was bigger than Dax by at least six inches and fifty pounds. Heavy brow and jaw, knotted knuckles, slightly bent nose—the guy looked like he'd seen too many rounds in the ring.

When the man stopped, his head twitching like a dog catching an interesting scent, Dax stepped further back into the empty office. He waited for the sound of boots stomping along the hallway and down the stairs before stepping out of his hiding place and returning to Mabon Enterprises' door. Holding his breath, he pressed his ear to the polished wood. The sound of muffled crying reached him through the door.

Dax clenched his hands hard enough that his knuckles popped. *Damn it!* He'd come to Mabon's office for one reason—to get his money from winning the night's fight. His striking coach had warned him not to get involved in the underground fight clubs, that they were the first step into a more dangerous world. But when Isadora Kane, CEO of Mabon Enterprises, had approached him after his last Brazilian jiu-jitsu tournament, her offer for a chance to fight for a tempting wad of cash had been impossible to resist.

And Ms. Kane had seemed trustworthy, hardly dangerous. More like a cougar—pretty, polished, flirty, rich—than an underground fight organizer. *Shit!* What if the guy he saw leaving had done something to Ms. Kane? What he'd hurt her?

Dax rapped his knuckles softly against the door, then pressed his ear to it again. Nothing. He tried the knob, a part of him hoping it'd be locked. But it turned, the clicking of the latch setting his nerves on edge.

"Hello?" he whispered as he peered into the dark

office. It took his eyes a moment to adjust once he shut the door behind him, cutting off the light from the hallway. "Anyone in here?"

No one spoke, but he could hear sobbed breaths coming from somewhere nearby. He crept slowly, trying not to smash his shins or trip over anything. Opening an unlocked door wasn't breaking and entering, right? Although, creeping around in the dark was likely to look suspicious to anyone who caught him. The last thing he wanted was to spend the night in lockup. Again.

He moved toward a door on the far side of the office, light leaking from under it. Once again, he pressed his ear to the wood and knocked softly. Someone on the other side made a surprised noise—a woman by the sound of it, probably the same one he'd heard crying.

"Hey, is someone in there?"

A woman replied. But her voice was muffled, so he couldn't understand what she said. When he turned the unlocked doorknob and pushed the door open, the light nearly blinded him. And once his eyes adjusted, he almost wished he had been.

The woman was around his age and sorority-girl pretty, clad in expensive-looking yoga clothes. That wasn't so weird—she could have been Ms. Kane's administrative assistant on her way to a class for all he knew. Except the woman wasn't going anywhere anytime soon because she was dangling like a fly from a spiderweb, nearly a foot above the desk. Someone, probably the big guy that had just left, had bound her arms and legs behind her with intricately knotted rope and strapped a leather blindfold-ball gag contraption onto her head.

Sweet baby Jesus, what kind of kinky shit did I just walk into?

He'd only seen anything like it in person once, when the last woman Jamie had set him up with had dragged him to a sex club. Not that he'd known where she was taking him—she'd said something about a great sushi place—or that Anchorage even had such a thing. Most awkward first—and last—date ever. It wasn't that he had a problem with a bit of pain or bondage between consenting adults, but the things he saw that night crossed a line he was happy to stay behind.

"Umm... I'm sorry. I'll just go." Dax stepped back through the doorway and nearly turned to leave, but there was something about the way the woman squirmed in her bindings that made him stop and ask, "Hey, umm... kind of a personal question, I know, but are you okay?"

The sound she made in reply made him think that she wasn't. He returned to her, keeping his eyes locked on her face. Anything else seemed pervy.

"I'm going to remove this mask thing, okay?"

When she nodded, he unhooked the buckles at the back of her head and peeled the contraption away. Bright blue eyes latched onto him, her mouth working frantically like she was trying to say something. *Weird. Maybe she isn't the woman I heard talking earlier.*

Dax peered around the room, confirming they were alone and looking for a bottle of water or something else for the woman to drink. Nothing. "Just shake your head for no and nod for yes. Do you need help?"

Her head bobbed.

Shit. Not the answer I was hoping for. "Okay. Just give me a minute to figure out how to untie you."

Dax tried to avoid touching her, but given how they'd tied her, it was impossible not to. The rope seemed to be a continuous length, and untying her was like trying to untangle Christmas lights already wrapped around a tree.

He was shoulder-deep in knotted rope when he heard a feminine huff that wasn't coming from the bound woman. Dax looked up to find Ms. Kane standing in the doorway. She looked less friendly than the last time he'd seen her. The huge guy he'd seen leaving earlier loomed behind her, looking like he wanted to rip Dax's head off.

"This isn't what it looks like," Dax said.

The woman arched a perfectly sculpted blonde eyebrow. "You're not trying to steal my hostage?"

"Your what?" Dax gaped at Ms. Kane for a moment. *Seriously, what kind of freaky shit did I stumble into?* "Look, I'm just here to get paid, but this woman seemed to need help. I was just trying to—"

"Aren't you just the handsome hero swooping in to rescue the damsel." The woman's laugh made him think of an over-the-top cartoon villain. She stepped to the side, gesturing for her companion to enter the room. "Dimitri, educate him about what happens to anyone who touches my property, then tries to blackmail me."

"Hold up! You've got it all wrong." Dax took a step back from the bound woman, raising his hands in front of him as he scanned the room for a way out. It had no windows—not that he could safely escape through one since they were on the third floor—and Ms. Kane and her goon blocked the only door. *Shit! I need to get out of here.* But he didn't feel right abandoning the woman. *Once I'm free, I'll call the cops to help her*, he silently vowed. "I didn't touch her. And I wasn't trying to blackmail you. I just wanted my purse from tonight's fight. I swear."

"I saw you touch her. Your filthy, mundane hands were all over her." Her cold green stare raked over him. "You humans are all the same. I thought you might be different. I certainly didn't expect you to win that match. I recruited you to play the sandbag." She reached out and patted the huge man's arm. "It seems I have a Solstice gift for you after all, Dimitri. Someone who might prove good hunting and actually put up a fight."

"Look, lady. I don't know what kind of thing you people have going on here. And to be honest, I don't care. If you're all consenting adults, well, who am I to say anything? Everyone has their kink, right?" No need for him to bring up that he doubted the younger woman was a willing participant. At least not with this audience.

Dax had been edging his way around the room as he talked, Ms. Kane's goon stalking him. Once he got to a spot where the dangling woman was between him and the big guy, his only obstacle through the door being Ms. Kane, he said, "Just hand over my purse and I'll leave. I won't say a word, and you never have to see me again."

"You're right about not saying a word," she replied with an overly sweet smile, gesturing for her man to move on him.

Dax evaded his grab and pushed past Ms. Kane, but he hardly made it a half dozen steps before he crashed into a second man, larger than the first. The brute grabbed him, bypassing Dax's attempt to pivot away. *How can such a big guy move so fast?*

The man wrapped an arm around Dax's throat, squeezing. Ducking his chin, Dax tried to keep the man from choking him. But the pressure was too much, threatening to dislocate his jaw and making his vision flicker.

Dax used every trick he knew to free himself— including a desperate shot at the man's balls—but failed. There was a huge difference between a sparring partner and a freakishly huge psycho trying to pop your head from your neck like a dandelion bloom. This guy wanted him dead.

Dax might have disagreed with the man's intent, but it was an argument he wasn't going to win. His world darkened at the edges. *Jamie always said playing the hero would get me killed...*

THAT DAX WOKE up alive surprised him. Well, he assumed he was alive. He doubted Hell would look and smell like the trunk of a car. Although, he'd always suspected bubblegum pop would be the Devil's version of elevator music. Stopping himself from yelling at his kidnappers to shut the shit off—not that he'd be able to get his complaints past the nasty-tasting cloth stuffed in his mouth—he tried to focus on wiggling his feet and hands. Nothing. It was like those parts of his body had disappeared.

Probably best not to follow that line of thought.

He drew his knees toward his chest and heard his shoes scraping against the inside of the trunk. When his knees bumped against something—Dax could only assume it was his hands—he felt a surge of fear at the lack of sensation. How long could circulation be cut off before he had permanent damage?

Raising his hands toward his face, he nuzzled at the cold, numb flesh. His nose bumped against eight fingers, two thumbs, and a narrow band of plastic locking his hands together. He felt a small amount of joy that his captors had bound his hands with a zip tie instead of rope or handcuffs. Zip ties could be broken without much effort, or so the self-defense instructor at his fight gym had claimed.

Dax rolled onto his back, wincing as what was probably a giant goose egg on the back of his skull pressed against the bottom of the trunk. He raised his wrists as high as they could go in the cramped confines, then brought them down slowly toward his chest, spreading his elbows to see how much room he had. Scooting an inch or two closer to what he assumed was the passenger part of the car, he repeated the process. Once he knew the paths of his elbows were clear, he raised his hands upward again, pulling them fast and hard toward his chest. It took a couple tries, but his hands finally broke free.

After several minutes of roughly rubbing his hands together and clenching and opening his fists, both burned with the pins and needles of returning circulation. Once he had enough feeling and dexterity back, he ripped the tape off his mouth and spat out the rag. For once, he was thankful for his inability to grow much of a beard.

Next on his to do list was freeing his feet. He slammed the edge of his joined hands against the zip tie circling his ankles until it snapped. Wiggling his feet as best he could, he tried not to cry out when the muscles in the soles seized up. When he curled his toes to stop the cramping, he was reminded that he'd left the house wearing sneakers, only planning to run a quick errand. No need to wear boots since he wouldn't be outside long enough for his toes to freeze.

Shit! That'll make things uncomfortable when I escape—cold feet and slippery soles. But at least he still had shoes. And clothes, except his coat. All things considered, he was lucky. His kidnappers could have stripped him down to his boxers to dump him in the middle of nowhere.

With a sigh, Dax fumbled along the back side of the trunk, searching for the emergency release. Once he found it, he pulled the handle. Gripping the rubber gasket seal to control the lid, he peered through the crack. It looked like they were outbound on the Glenn Highway. And since there wasn't another car in sight, it was probably well past bar closing time.

As desperate as he was to escape his moving coffin, he couldn't jump from the car while it was speeding down the highway. He'd have to wait until it slowed down. Not that he was looking forward to that either. Road rash was a bitch. This time of year, a mixture of gravel and ice covered most roads, which would tear through his T-shirt and jeans and shred his skin like he was naked.

He gripped the edge of the tarp he was lying on, pulling it around his shoulders like a cape. Tarps, duct tape, and flares were an important part of any Alaskan vehicle's survival kit. Too bad he only had one of the three. It wouldn't do much to shield him, but it was better than nothing.

The trick would be not getting hurt during his escape. The timing would have to be perfect, jumping once the car had nearly come to a stop, but before anyone got out.

There was another choice—wait for the car to stop and the trunk to open, then fight off his kidnappers—but there were too many problems with that. What if they were armed? Or the huge goons from the office? He'd be kissing his ass goodbye before he even got out of the trunk. No, as much as he hated to admit it, his best bet was to run. He pulled the trunk lid closed, then settled in to wait, preserving his strength and energy.

When the car veered to the right, Dax assumed it was to leave the highway, and he cracked the lid again. He recognized the distinctive layout of the exit: Thunderbird Falls. He barely got the lid closed again before sliding across the trunk as the car took the sharp curve too fast. He braced himself as it fishtailed again on the turn for the road up to Eklutna Lake.

The meager contents of his stomach lurched, threatening to come back up as the car sped through the twists, dips, and rises of the narrow road. But he clung to a thread of hope. If his kidnappers were taking him all the way to the lake, he had a couple options once he escaped. He knew that area well, could find shelter at a public use cabin or nearby house. His friend Toby had a place just a couple miles from the lake. He was in Colorado visiting his folks for the holidays, but if Dax made it there, he'd be able to telephone for help. Dax wrapped the tarp tighter around his shoulders and tried to breathe through growing nausea.

The car slowed, the sound of the tires changing from the crunching of icy gravel to the muted creaking of just snow. *Time to make a break for it.* Sucking in a deep breath, Dax raised the trunk lid, gripped the edges of the tarp—his only protection from the cold and snow—and jumped. His feet hit the ground with a bone-jarring thud, and he rolled into the impact. As he got his feet back under him, he saw the taillights of the car brighten.

Running as fast as the slippery soles of his sneakers would allow, he darted for the relative safety of the woods. As he crashed through the brush, holding tight to the tarp, he heard two men shouting in Russian. Probably Dimitri and his big brother, fellow goon, whatever. Would they follow him into the woods? He couldn't imagine they'd bring him all this way only to let him escape now.

The hairs on the back of his neck rose like the Devil was breathing down it. His heart beat wildly, driving him to run. *Prey.* The word popped into his head, but instead of fueling his feet, it slowed them.

What am I doing? Dax didn't run from a fight. He hadn't run from his foster father, he hadn't run from taking responsibility for beating the man bloody, and he hadn't run from the assholes who tried to bully him in juvie. Hell, he hadn't even run from that brown bear on the Rover's Run trail. Admittedly, the goons from the Mabon Enterprises office were each the size of a bear, but they were still just men.

He slowed his run to a jog, taking in his surroundings. Maybe he could find some way to get the jump on these guys, take them out one at a time, then double back and take their car.

He couldn't see much in the light of the waning moon. The stark, straight trunks of spruce and birch trees surrounded him. The winter air was cold, crisp. His breathing sounded loud and ragged, wreathing his head in puffs of steam.

Dax took a deep breath that burned his throat and left his lungs aching with its chill. He held it for a count of five before letting it out slowly. He needed to calm down and think. Hell, he didn't even know which direction he was running anymore, and his feet and hands—his entire body, really—had passed the point of numb.

Maybe I should find a place to hunker down until morning. But if he stopped and curled up inside the tarp, it would probably end up being his death shroud.

A branch snapped to his left. He froze in place, holding his breath. It could be anything—the cold, a bird, something small and furry in the bushes, something not so cute and harmless. Another branch broke behind him. Too close. He spun toward the sound, his heart pounding.

The forest around him was filled with shadows—a downed tree here, a bush there. But everything was still. Wood cracked behind him. Again, he spun to find nothing but the woods. Despite all the trees, he'd never felt so exposed. Maybe he needed to make like a squirrel, find somewhere to hide.

He hunched under the tarp as he turned in a slow circle, figuring out his next move. *Please, whatever power out there in the universe that might be listening, I know I never pray, but if you could just help a guy out and get me through this, I'll—*

The creak of wood spun him again. Golden eyes flashed at head height from just a few feet away. A small shadow perched on a still-swaying branch, the eyes blinking slowly, then opening wide and round.

Just an owl. Dax willed his heart to beat again.

"I don't suppose you can you lead me to safety, little guy?" Dax whispered, chuckling darkly to himself. If only it could be that easy.

When the bird launched itself into the night sky on silent wings, some part of him went with it. He took a shuffling step to follow. But before he had the chance to take another, something heavy barreled into his back, knocking him to the snow.

He shook his head and drew in a pained breath. For a heartbeat, he flashed back to his past run-in with a bear, a similar wild, musky smell—strong enough he could practically taste it—filling his nose. Instinct drew his knees to his chest and arms around his head. He yanked the tarp over him, like a kid trying to hide under the covers from the monster in the closet, just as a heavy weight landed on him again.

Claws scraped against the stiff material of the tarp and a low growl filled the air. No, not a bear. It sounded more like a dog. An enormous, angry dog. The hell if he was going to let some hungry, mangy stray take him down. He hollered a string of curses as he rolled, knocking the beast from his back. Clambering to his feet, he held the tarp in front of him like a shield.

He wasn't sure what he expected to see—maybe a half-starved, matted mutt or something. But the beast growling in front of him wasn't like any dog he'd seen. Wolf? He didn't know they got so big. The creature must have weighed as much as Dax, if not more. Narrowed eyes glinted green, white fangs flashed in a vicious snarl, and silvery hackles raised.

Well, fuck.

Dax took a step back, then another, silently praying that he didn't trip over anything. He needed to find a tree to climb to get out of the wolf's reach, but he didn't dare take his eyes off the beast. It slowly stalked in his wake, apparently in no hurry to take him down again.

It was like the beast was taunting him, trying to scare him. And it was succeeding. Its toothy snarl was just as intimidating as the bear's had been, a stark reminder that there were things above Dax in the food chain.

Over the summer, Dax had heard about a guy who'd successfully fought off a brown bear by punching it in the snout. Would that work on a wolf? He was about to find out. The beast wasn't backing off, and Dax wasn't going down without a fight.

A loud growl sounded at Dax's back. He spun, locking eyes with a second, darker furred wolf. *Shit! Two of the fucking things?* He was such an idiot. Wolves weren't like bears. They traveled in packs. Were there others, waiting for him to fall?

All Dax could do was mutter one last prayer—one that ended with "time to kiss my ass goodbye"—as he kept his eyes pinned to the wolves. He crouched, hunching his shoulders and balling his fists. No fucking way he'd be an easy meal.

"Come and get me, bitches."

CHAPTER 3

ZELDA WAS IN A DARK MOOD. DESPITE COMPLETING Isadora's mission, the high priestess had declared it a failure. Her reason? Jonah, a resident spirit at the Anchorage Hotel, hadn't overheard what the woman had hoped for. Not that Zelda or Jonah had any control over what the men in Room 205 said. It was just another excuse for Isadora to keep Larissa away from Coven House for Solstice.

It was impossible to feel festive without her sister there. Feast and ritual weren't the same without her. It had been a relief when Isadora dismissed Zelda to her room. *Goddess forbid I ruin Her Highness, Most Beauteous and Benevolent, Queen Isadora's mood with my 'pouting.'*

The owl that lighted on the cottonwood branch outside Zelda's bedroom window carried ominous news. Images flashed through her mind through her connection to her familiar—stark trees, wolves circling, blood on the snow, shredded cloth and skin, dirt scattering over a tarp, the sign for the Eklutna Lake Campground.

Shit! Had Isadora's werewolves killed? Someone had been dumped in a shallow grave near Eklutna Lake. "Who?" she whispered to her familiar, Minnie, but the owl only silently urged her to hurry and flew off into the night.

If Isadora unleashed the wolves on Larissa as punishment...

A cold pit opened in Zelda's belly, the pressure in her chest making it difficult to breathe. She'd been dreading this, sure that the escalating tension would end in someone's death. As a precaution, she'd gathered and stockpiled supplies for a resurrection ritual, based on her grandmother's experiments and carefully scrawled notes in her grimoire. But she'd prayed to the Goddess that she'd never have to use them. She hastily grabbed the supplies as she willed her life-challenged friend Billie to join her.

The spirit appeared in the center of the room, her eyebrows arching as she watched Zelda stuffing her backpack. "What has happened, mistress?"

"What have I told you about calling me that?" Zelda asked. Not that she truly wanted an answer. Billie and the other spirits' use of the title was disturbing, making her feel like she'd enslaved them. "Minnie showed me that the werewolves killed someone tonight. I need a distraction so I can go see for myself."

"You believe it is Larissa? You intend to attempt your ritual?" When Zelda nodded, cinching her backpack to her body, the spirit continued. "The high priestess recently replaced your great-grandmother's portrait above the mantle with her own. I have been looking for an excuse to express my opinion."

"Have fun. And be careful."

The spirit offered a sweet smile, gingerly patted the finger curls of her chin-length bob, then disappeared. Within moments, she heard the wolves' gruff shouts and shattering glass. *That's my cue.*

She climbed out her window and down the cottonwood tree, then hurried toward her car as fast she could in the knee-deep snow. Once again, she was in Billie's debt, a tab that had escalated out of control since Isadora had become high priestess of the coven.

The chill in her belly only grew as she drove to the lake as fast as the icy roads would allow. This was all her fault. How many times had Isadora warned Zelda there would be consequences for failure? And what had Zelda been thinking to argue with the woman when she'd declared this last mission one? She'd been an idiot to let frustration run her mouth. If anything happened to Larissa because she'd provoked the high priestess....

Zelda drove into the empty park, following the tire tracks in the day-old snow. They stopped at the day camping area. Her insides felt as icy as the winter air when she parked and trudged to her Subaru's back hatch. Popping it open, she grabbed her down jacket and skirt, zipping herself into both before perching on the bumper to pull on her boots. The bone-chilling temperatures wouldn't warm until hours after sunrise. Resurrecting the dead would be impossible if she was a witch-cicle.

Her mind wandered as she loaded her supplies onto a

small sled. *Flaming hells, am I actually doing this?* What would Larissa say? Probably, "The dead are that way for a reason," followed by, "Don't play God." Would she forgive Zelda for bringing her back?

What if the wolves' victim wasn't Larissa? It wasn't like she could dig up the body, see it wasn't her sister, and walk away. There was another possibility—she could still raise whoever it was, ask them to help her. Most people would pay any price for a second chance at life, right? And getting Larissa back was all that mattered.

Isadora had driven Zelda to this, to crossing a line she'd never wanted to. While she'd spent years researching her grandmother's notes and months developing a resurrection ritual, it was only theory. Now that she was here, preparing to haul her supplies to a fresh grave and dig up a corpse, it was disturbingly real. She was about to become the monster they'd all feared she'd become—the mad sorceress digging up corpses, violating the natural law that the dead stay that way.

And it could all be for nothing. What would she do if the resurrection ritual didn't work? Or even worse, just raised a shambling corpse as her grandmother's experiments had done? Zelda hadn't worked up the fortitude to run her own trials. At worst, she might have to slay a zombie, one who could be her sister; at best, she'd have to build a funeral pyre. She couldn't leave a body for someone to stumble across. That would surely get the attention of Council Enforcers, and no one wanted that.

It wasn't her thoughts or the cold that sent a shiver racing up her spine, but an arriving spirit. Anticipation had her wound tight, and she couldn't stop the shriek that escaped when the ghost appeared in front of her. Not that there was anything remotely frightening about the semitransparent woman.

"Billie! What are you doing here? Why aren't you at Coven House?"

If it was possible for a spirit to blanch, this one managed it, her image flickering. "Mistress, I caused a ruckus 'til I could no longer. But High Priestess Isadora attempted to banish me." The ghost squared her slender shoulders, her eyes glinting with pride. "I waited 'til just the right moment to retreat to you. She likely thinks she was successful in her efforts."

"Damn it, stop calling me that!" Zelda grumped. "Isadora was still there?"

"My apologies, miss—" The spirit made a noise like she was sucking in a noisy breath, her form dimming again. "Unfortunately, Isadora has discovered that you departed Coven House. Although she appeared to believe Miss Lucy's claim that you had snuck away to see a lover."

"A lover? What the hells was Lucy thinking?"

Depending on what happened in the next few hours, Lucy was either a genius or an idiot. If Larissa was in the grave, and Zelda succeeded in resurrecting her, they could easily disappear and Isadora might blame it on this lover. But if the body belonged to someone else and Zelda had to rescue Larissa from Isadora afterward, the woman would spare no energy looking for this secret lover to abuse as punishment. And when she didn't find him and learned Lucy had lied, her coven sister's life would be in danger.

Curse Isadora! And curse her father for leaving Zelda and Larissa to deal with the woman after he'd fled to London to bed and wed a new, less troublesome high priestess! The man was clearly counting his new heirs before they hatched.

She gave herself a moment to wallow in self-pity and anger before she took a deep breath and forced herself to focus. Billie might be a trusted ally, but it was dangerous for a necromancer to lose herself to emotions. Less benevolent spirits could exploit that kind of inner turmoil.

Zelda knew the dangers. A vengeful spirit had possessed her grandmother, exploiting the woman's loss of control after she'd discovered her husband in bed with another witch. The resulting abomination had murdered the adulterers and torched Coven House before the witches could stop her. Was it any wonder that Zelda's mother had abandoned her when they'd discovered she also had an affinity for the dead?

As for her grandmother, the coven had magically bound her, locking her away for nearly a decade until Zelda finally had the skill and power to exorcise the spirit. Not that the woman had survived for long afterward, her own spirit weakened beyond healing.

Strength, skill, power, luck. Based on what little her grandmother and Franklin—the bane of her existence— had taught her, she'd need them all to resurrect the dead. Once Death sank his bony fingers into a spirit, he didn't give it up without a fight.

Zelda's gaze swept the parking area, looking for the owl. She'd find the burial site faster with her familiar as a guide. She closed her eyes and gazed skyward, willing Minnie to appear.

"I can take you," Billie said in a quiet voice, interrupting the summoning. "I can feel it. The spirit is restless, angry."

"I'm not surprised. I'd be pissed too. Stupid werewolves."

The hoot of an owl sounded near the trailhead, and Zelda headed toward it. Billie fell in at her flank, her energy growing chaotic as they neared the woods. Zelda hadn't planned on summoning the spirit for help, knowing this task would strike a bit close to home—a werewolf had brought her end as well, nearly a century before. "You don't need to come. I know this is hard for you."

"Who better?" Billie's ghostly hand hovered near Zelda's cheek, not quite completing the tender gesture. "You are gifted. Maybe you will be able to accomplish what your grandmother could not. I wish to bear witness. Do not deny me the small amount of peace that snatching this victim from Death's jaws will bring me."

"I'm glad to have you at my side," Zelda conceded. Billie had been Zelda's first spirit companion, a ghostly nanny since her earliest memories. The dead woman had been more of a mother than the woman who'd birthed her. "Can you tell if it's Larissa?"

Zelda had kept her gaze focused on the trail and Minnie's winged form guiding her down it, but when

Billie didn't answer right away, she chanced a glance in the spirit's direction.

Billie's brow furrowed in concentration, a frown tugging at her lips as she shook her head. "I do not think it is. This spirit yearns for blood and battle. Larissa has never been a fighter."

Zelda extended her own spirit outward, searching past the ancient ones who called this place home. With an exceptional effort of will, she kept from cringing away when she found the newest ghostly denizen. Vengeful would be one way to describe it, but the word was woefully inadequate. The spiritual pressure felt like that moment just before an explosion. This was a poltergeist in the making, craving destruction.

Billie was right. It was unlikely the spirit was Larissa. Her sister had never fought for anything in her life. She was as gentle and timid as a bunny. Yet the energy reaching Zelda told her this spirit was no stranger to violence.

Zelda should have been relieved that her sister likely wasn't in that grave. But if she was alive, it meant she was still Isadora's hostage and the nightmare would only continue.

Could she—*should* she—harness this spirit and return it to its vessel? Convince it to help her, turn its anger toward their common enemy—Isadora and her werewolves? The last time she'd bound a violent spirit, she'd ended up regretting it.

When Minnie left the trail, Zelda followed. Uneven ground and deeper snow slowed her travel. The sled jolted and dipped behind her, occasionally snagging on brush and obstructions just under the snow. She walked in silence for what seemed like hours, the spirit luring her like a beacon. Finally, Minnie landed on the upended roots of a downed tree.

Even if Minnie hadn't signaled that they'd reached their destination, she'd have known the body was there. Not only could she sense the icy hand of Death, but a roughly person-sized patch of disturbed earth darkened the snow where the old tree once stood. Near its center, the spirit lingered, still clinging to its vessel with an angry tether, one that would grow more brittle as sunrise neared.

Spirits took several paths once freed from their vessel. Some passed through the barrier to their afterlife, someplace Zelda knew little about since she'd never encountered a spirit who had returned from there. Sometimes spirits lingered in a place between, not ready to move on. Those tended to watch, rather than participate in, the affairs of the living. Some, like Billie, continued in the realm of the living, generally ignoring that their corporeal existence had ended, lingering near people and places that were familiar and linked to their old life. And some, like Franklin, remained only to torment the living and bring chaos to the world—jealous, angry, bitter. Once a spirit entered that state, it was nearly impossible to redeem it.

Not that Zelda hadn't tried.

"It is dangerous." Billie hung back, her expression wistful as she stared at the formless spirit. As always, the woman was her voice of reason. "You are playing with fire to attempt this."

"How can I not? The connection between the spirit and its vessel is weakening faster than I expected." Zelda could feel it—the spirit was strong, but having one's life snuffed in such an unexpected and violent way took a toll. She was sure that true resurrection would be impossible once the connection between body and soul shattered. Her grandmother had managed to reanimate corpses, cramming a spirit into an empty vessel. But the body and mind always continued to deteriorate, until all that remained was a mindless zombie. "I might have to use a binding spell to strengthen the connection."

Billie's eyes widened as she stared at Zelda. "You would bind that spirit to your own? It is too dangerous. Once you open the barrier to your own vessel, the spirit could overwhelm you, take control. Look at what happened the last time—"

"So, I won't let it," Zelda cut Billie off, unwilling to rehash the old arguments about Franklin. Yes, she'd screwed up by ignoring Billie's advice to banish the spirit, but this time she'd make sure she was the only one to suffer the consequences.

"You already risk too much with this ritual. But if you bind this spirit to your own and do not return it to its vessel by morning's light, you risk your own soul."

"Then I guess I'll have to succeed, won't I?" Zelda raised her hand to silence any further arguments. "If it puts you at ease, I'll only do it as a last resort. And I promise I'll be careful."

Zelda turned her attention to her preparations. She unloaded the Yule log—a portion of an ash trunk, cut on its top edge like a cross to allow it to burn for hours—from the sled. Like her coven sisters, she'd prepared her log earlier in the day for the Solstice celebration. Luckily, the herbs she'd stuffed into the incisions would also work for the resurrection.

She set the Yule log at the north end of the grave, then pulled candles from her backpack, placing them in the cardinal directions. Lighting her smudge stick, she circled the clearing, taking care to keep Billie outside it and the other spirit within it. For the moment, the shapeless thing stalked between the downed tree and its vessel, but that was likely to change once she excavated the body. Spirits reacted to seeing their vessels in different ways—the shock could solidify or disperse it. Yet another reason to bind the spirit to herself.

With one last hoot, Minnie took refuge in a tree at the edge of the clearing. Billie moved to stand next to the owl, both creatures watching her with round, glowing eyes. Zelda took a deep breath, whispering a prayer to the Goddess as she lit the candles and the Yule log, then closed the circle with an effort of will.

She knelt alongside the grave near the burning log, pulling off her gloves before pressing her hands into the dirt. The loose soil had started to refreeze, its edges sharp with sticks and rocks. It would have been less damaging to dig with the shovel or with her gloves on, but then it wouldn't be so easy to feel if she reached the body. She'd pushed in up to her elbows before her fingertips scraped against something that wasn't dirt, likely the tarp from her vision.

The wolves hadn't buried the body deeply. Zelda pulled free from the dirt and pushed herself to her feet, rubbing her hands on the stiff shell of her down skirt before pulling her gloves back on. She retrieved the shovel, pressing its square edge into the dirt where her arm had been moments before.

After removing nearly a foot of loose dirt, she dropped to her knees again near the Yule log and pulled off her gloves. Her hands didn't burrow far before encountering the shroud again. It covered something hard, rounded. A head?

She dug quickly with her hands, exposing a length of tarp. *Please don't let the vessel be too badly damaged.* Wolves weren't exactly known for being neat and tidy in their kills. And if they'd torn into the body's soft belly...

Bile rose in Zelda's throat, her hand shaking as it gripped the tarp. She took a long, stuttering breath, then looked up to find the spirit hovering a bit closer, amorphous and tense.

"You don't need to be afraid. I'm here to help." Again, there was a surge of anger, although it didn't feel directed at her. She spoke in her most soothing tone. "I promise. I mean no harm. At least not toward you." *If you behave.*

The spirit moved closer and she could feel its slight shift in mood, uncertainty joining the anger. Zelda needed to stay calm. If she did, the spirit would be more likely to do the same. Hopefully.

No more stalling. It was time to see what she was going to be working with. She peeled back the tarp and peered into the shallow grave. Her heart clenched, and she sucked in a breath. The body belonged to a man. And not just any man, but the mysterious dark-haired fighter.

"Dax Rand. How did you end up here?" But dead

bodies didn't speak, and his spirit was mute, still too confused to take form and consciousness.

Zelda peered toward the east. Sunrise was coming. She needed to be ready with the invocation when the first rays of morning hit. She climbed to her feet as she pulled her gloves back on, retrieved the shovel, and began chiseling away at the grave's edges. She needed to widen the hole so she'd have better access to the body.

Eventually, she'd widened the grave so she had space for a makeshift altar, as well as room to maneuver. The flickering flames cast shadows through the clearing, the light dancing across the body. Zelda stepped down into the grave, setting her open backpack on its lip.

She sent her gaze over the man's wounds. The wolves had done considerable damage—deep punctures on his neck, scratches and bite marks along his tattooed arms and chest, and a tear along one of his thighs. They hadn't marred his face, but his expression was fierce—lips pulled back in a snarl, dark eyes narrowed. When she rolled his stiff body, she saw long, parallel tears running from shoulders to hips.

It could be worse. At least all his parts were still attached, and his vital organs remained tucked out of sight where they belonged.

As she reached out to smooth away his snarl and shut his eyes, she peered up at the hovering spirit. His movement along the edge of the grave looked like pacing, reminding her of Dax's earlier movements in the fight cage. The way he was focused on her left her feeling like if she moved wrong, he'd pounce.

Zelda pulled healing tincture, hemp bandages, and

medical tape from her pack and began the process of cleaning and wrapping his wounds. Death and the cold might have stopped them from bleeding, but if all went well, that would be a temporary state.

As she widened the rips in his T-shirt and the leg of his jeans, she reassured the spirit, "Don't worry. No funny business here. I'm just taking care of these wounds. We don't want you bleeding out before we get you out of here."

Zelda let the words continue to flow, not much worrying about their content, just her tone. Calm, soothing, like one would speak to a skittish stray.

By the time she'd finished the bandaging, the sky was brightening to the east. She looked up to find the spirit had stopped pacing and was now hovering, watchful, and perhaps curious.

There wasn't much time to finish preparations. She turned to her backpack and unloaded her ritual supplies —a pair of silver bowls, a half dozen carefully labeled vials and bottles of various sizes, a fist-sized chunk of bloodstone, a baggie filled with herbs, and an elaborately embroidered altar cloth. She also pulled out her burning bundle—various woods and herbs wrapped in a braided red, green, and white ribbon.

An expectant calm descended as she rolled out her altar cloth, then carefully placed every item and filled the silver bowls, one with milk and honey and the other with spiced apple cider. The scents of her herbs— frankincense, myrrh, eucalyptus, cinnamon, and sandalwood—tickled her nose, filling her with anticipation.

As the sun's rays began to peek above the mountains, she placed the burning bundle into the Yule log's flames and opened the vial of anointing oil. She dabbed her finger into it and drew a sigil on the man's forehead, over his heart, and on his belly. A shiver passed through her as she dug under her layers of clothing, icy fingers blindly replicating the designs on herself.

The oil tingled, an icy heat on her skin. The log's fire flared as she tossed a handful of ground herbs at it. Some were still sticking to her palm when she laid it over the man's heart and began her invocation.

"Queen of Heaven, One Who is All, I beseech thee. Allow this man's spirit to return to its vessel. Grant this humble servant the power to breathe his life, his spirit, back into him. As the Oak King, the Sun, is reborn with sunrise, so too be Dax Rand."

She took a deep breath as the first rays of morning hit them. *Now or never.* She opened herself, drawing the spirit into her body as she drank from the silver bowl with the cider.

Zelda had only let two spirits enter her during her lifetime: Billie and Franklin. Billie's spirit was filled with loyalty, affection, a motherly concern and care. Franklin's was dark to her light, filled with anger, frustration, and fear. She could feel those same things in Dax's, but his had something both had lacked. Wonder. And under it all was a seemingly bottomless well of love for family, friends, and life.

She fought back the urge, one she suspected was not coming from her, to throw back her head and howl into the brightening morning sky from the injustice of a life cut tragically and unexpectedly short. She hardly knew the man, but it suddenly seemed very important that she keep him among the living, with her. Her spirit reached out, wrapping around Dax's, to soothe and comfort. *Please. We can help each other*.

"Goddess, grant me this wish. Make him whole."

She leaned over him and sucked in a deep breath, one that left her lungs feeling like they'd burst. After taking another sip of cider, she molded her lips to his and let the tart liquid dribble into his mouth. Her spirit unraveled from his as she exhaled it into him. She could almost see its light filling every cell of his body.

At first, she thought she was imagining that his lips no longer felt so hard and cold against hers. But as she pulled away, chilled fingers threaded into her hair, drawing her back down. She heard a ragged intake of breath but wasn't sure which one of them took it. Maybe both. His lips moved hungrily as he deepened the kiss, the tip of his tongue finding hers. It tasted of cider.

Either she'd succeeded in bringing Dax back from the dead, or she'd raised a zombie and was about to get her face eaten off. When she drew back and opened her eyes, his blinked back at her, clearly startled and confused but bright with life.

A smile curled her lips. She'd done it.

"Welcome back, Dax Rand."

CHAPTER 4

In his twenty-five years of life, Dax had never cried. At least not that he remembered. But when the angel's soft lips parted from his and her gentle hands withdrew from his face, he did. Hot, silent tears that tickled their way into his hairline. He'd sell his soul to feel her touch again.

Dax peered skyward, holding his breath as he reached a numb hand toward the angel leaning over him. His fingertips brushed her cheek, the contact sending a warm tingle down his arm that settled in his chest. She was real.

Blinking, he rubbed at his burning eyes with his other hand. His angel's face was pale as the moon, her blonde hair shining silver in its light. But his touch had left a smudge of dirt on her cheek, bringing her down to earth.

As did her words. "Shit. You're getting dirt in your eyes." She pulled her sleeve down over her hand, then swiped it across his face. The gesture reminded him of his sister Jennie with her kids—sweet even as she scolded.

He tried to speak, but his throat was raw, like he'd been screaming for hours. When he gingerly cleared it, sympathetic eyes met his. She cautiously explored the torn skin of his knuckles with her fingertips before gripping his wrists and pulling him into a sitting position.

"Take it slow. You've been dead for hours. From what I understand, souls do more damage going in than coming out." She wrapped a wool blanket around his shoulders, the fibers rough against his exposed skin and the sharp lanolin smell making him want to sneeze.

"Dead? Soul?" he croaked. "Who—"

"Well, you were only mostly dead. And mostly dead is still partly alive." She winked. "You can call me Miracle Max."

Did angels have a sense of humor? Doubtful. "Did you just quote a kids' movie to me?"

The woman sat back on her heels, frowning as she crossed her arms over her chest. "*The Princess Bride* is not a 'kids' movie.' It's a classic. Don't make me regret raising you from the dead."

"Or the mostly dead."

The woman gave a surprised chuckle. "Right. You catch on quick. You're coping with this better than I'd expected. I know it's only been a few minutes, but do you think you can get up and walk? We need to find someplace warm. There's a public use cabin a mile or so southeast of here."

"Wait," he whispered, studying the darkness around them. It stunk of wolves, the wild scent stronger than the candles, log, and whatever else she'd been burning. Didn't she notice it? "You shouldn't be here. The wolves—"

"Are long gone."

"How do you—"

"Because their car is gone."

Dax gaped at the woman, her words jumbled in his head. He shook it, as though that could knock some sense into him. "Their what?"

"Look, it's a long story. Once we get someplace warm, have a stiff drink or two, I'll tell you all about it. It'll be a good distraction while I stitch you up."

"Stitch me up?"

She sighed, dragging pale fingers through shimmering hair. "This must be freaking you out. One minute you've got a wolf latched to your throat, and the next you're waking up in a shallow grave. Will it get you moving if I give you a quick summary?"

"Couldn't hurt." To be honest, Dax wasn't convinced this wasn't a nightmare. Or maybe Hell. "Start with who you are and how you found me."

She looked surprised, like he should know. "My name is Zelda Melik. An owl, my familiar, told me you were here." She hurried to explain, not that what she said next was any more believable. "She told me that Isadora's wolves had killed someone and buried them here. I found you, dug you out, cleaned and bandaged your wounds, and put your soul back in your body. And now here we are. Can we please go?"

"Oh, that makes perfect sense," Dax muttered. While Zelda had been talking, he'd been trying to convince his body that it was time to get up and go. It ignored him. He frowned down at his numb and unmoving legs and feet. "Getting out of here is a great idea, but there's a problem." He waved a hand over his motionless legs. "You wouldn't happen to be hiding a wheelbarrow and a giant, would you?"

"Nope, just little ol' me and a kiddie sled." She nibbled at her lip as she joined him in frowning at his lower half. "Hmm... Let me know when you feel something."

He watched Zelda squeeze his toes through his sneakers, then pinch her way up his legs. Her cheeks flushed when she reached his thighs, the pink darkening to red as she poked and prodded her way past his hips. But he felt nothing.

"There." He couldn't help but flinch when her hand reached his bruised ribs. *Fuck! Am I paralyzed?* He stared down at his feet, willing them to move. Nothing.

"Goddess." Zelda released the word on an exhale, then chewed her lip for a moment. She muttered apologies whenever he flinched during her exploration up and down his spine, growing quiet when he stopped reacting at a point below the waistband of his jeans. When her fingers threaded into the hair at the nape of his neck, following his neck vertebrae toward his shoulders, a tingling jolted downward.

"I don't feel anything out of place or obviously broken. Maybe your numbness is temporary, from swelling and trauma."

"Trauma... I guess that's a polite way of saying I got fucked up by a couple of mangy mutts."

Her hand slowly withdrew, rearranging the blanket around his shoulders, then tugging at the tarp under him. "We can use this as a sled of sorts, since you're too big for the one I brought. I think we're almost halfway between the cabin and my car, which is probably the better choice."

"If you could just take me to the hospital, they can patch me up and send me home."

"Umm... that's not a good idea. The hospital will ask too many questions. And if word gets out about a wolf attack up here, well..." She sighed. "I can't let that happen. And it's too dangerous for you to go home. They probably think you're dead, but there's no guarantee they aren't watching your house, your family, girlfriend, whatever." The woman peered at him from beneath long lashes, a finger twisting a lock of blonde hair. "I mean, Isadora knows where you live, right? You probably filled something out that had your address, or gave her a copy of your driver's license or something before your fight."

"Underground fight clubs aren't usually big on checking IDs or filing tax paperwork. It's a cash business, one where you can tell them your name is Bozo von Clownfuck and they don't care." Dax was quickly realizing how cold he was. "I need to call my brother. He was only expecting me to be gone for an hour. He's probably called out a search party by now."

"Weren't you listening? It's probably best if you disappear for a bit, until after..." She gave him an assessing look, then tightened the blanket around his shoulders. "Let me clean everything up and we'll get out of here, to wherever I'm going to stash you until we're ready."

"Ready?"

"Don't worry about it. Like I said, I'll fill you in on the details once we're someplace warm."

Before he could stop himself, he blurted, "My buddy has a place a mile or so outside the park. He won't be home for a couple weeks, so we'd have the place to ourselves."

"That should work."

When had this become 'we' and 'our'? Dax didn't know this woman. And she had to be crazy, claiming she'd brought him back from the dead, that Ms. Kane had sent wolves after him. None of this made sense.

He watched Zelda climb to her feet and stretch. She might not be an actual angel, but she had a unique sort of beauty and grace. Eyes the color of the morning sky peered at him from an ivory face, cheeks pink from the cold. There was something familiar about her... something he couldn't place.

She flashed him a nervous smile, like they were in a bar and she'd just caught him checking her out, and busied herself with gathering her things. Dax continued to watch her, trying to distract himself from the pins-and-needles sensation crawling under the skin he could feel. Maybe it was a side effect of having been mostly dead. Or maybe it was whatever she'd put on the pungent bandages. The urge to peek beneath them left his fingers twitching against the cloth, but the damage was probably bad enough without him messing with them.

Damaged. He stared down at his deadened feet, once

again trying to will them to move. Nothing. "It might have been better if you'd left me dead."

Zelda's huff sounded annoyed as she slid into the hole and folded the tarp back over him. "Dead is never better. The spirits would be the first to tell you that. Your wounds will heal, and this"—she gestured at his motionless legs—"is probably temporary."

"Probably?"

"I don't know. This isn't what I expected. But I'm going to fix everything. I promise." If the determination on her face was any indication, she'd keep that promise.

Grabbing hold of the edge of the tarp, she began to tug. If he'd been feeling sorry for himself before, watching the slender woman fight to drag him from his grave while he did nothing made it worse. When he tried to roll over, planning to drag himself out like the top half of a zombie, she pressed him onto his back.

"For fuck's sake, stop being stubborn. I'm stronger than I look, but you're making this harder. Didn't you ever play 'light as a feather, stiff as a board' when you were a kid?" Something in his face must have told her that he'd no idea what she was talking about. "Just focus on being still and stiff, like a board, but your body being weightless. We've got a long way to go, and I don't want to burn through my reserves right at the start."

He'd never been the type to lie back and let someone else do all the work. And he really didn't want to start now, not with her. But he'd have to. It wasn't like he was going to drag his mangled body through a mile of frozen dirt and snow. As much as he hated to admit it, he needed her.

Dax closed his eyes, wrapping the blanket and tarp more tightly around himself. "Fine. I'll just lie here and be useless."

Her warm hand pressed against his cheek, a small smile turning the corners of her mouth upward. "You won't be for long."

ZELDA PARKED her car alongside the chalet-style house, trying not to weep at the sight of the steep stairs leading to the front door. Her whole body ached. She didn't have anything left. Maybe they could just stay in the car. Or keep driving down the mountain and find a handicap-accessible motel in Palmer or Wasilla.

"You didn't say anything about stairs."

"I didn't think about it," Dax grumbled from the back of the car. "You don't need to drag me up them. The key is taped inside the opening of the kayak hanging under the porch. Let yourself in, then head down into the basement and pop open the window nearest the car. You can pull me through it."

"Yeah, great plan. More dragging." Zelda sucked in a deep breath, then exited the car. *No point in quitting now.* The key was right where Dax said. She peeled it free, then climbed the snow-covered wooden stairs to the front door. Letting herself in, she flipped the light switch inside the doorway and kicked off her boots. Despite the large windows and the sun being up, little natural light was getting in.

The house was small, most of it visible from the front

door, but the vaulted ceiling opened it up. It wasn't what she expected—instead of frat boy chic, it was homey. A wood stove sat at one end of the great room, next to stairs heading up to a loft. Three doorways led off the open concept kitchen: one to an office, another to a bathroom, and the third to a steep set of stairs descending into the basement. So many stairs—was the architect M.C. Escher or something.

Her knees ached and her thighs burned as she descended into the basement. Dax's friend had set it up as a media room, a total man cave with its enormous sectional couch and gleaming wooden bar with matching stools. He'd painted the entire wall at the front of the house white—Zelda guessed it was for use with a projector. An eclectic mix of sports paraphernalia and fight posters covered the rest of the walls.

She moved to the window nearest her car, stepping up onto the couch to draw up the blinds and open it. The good news was that she could pull Dax through the window and right onto the couch. It was a drop of a couple feet, but likely not the worst thing he'd experienced in the last twenty-four hours. The bad news was that pulling Dax onto the couch would ruin the upholstery. The tarp was filthy. And even if she left it outside, Dax was covered in dirt and blood. The space might scream man cave, but it was an exceptionally clean one.

She took a moment to check out the rest of the basement. Similar to the main level of the house, another trio of doors led from the room. One went to a bathroom that was little more than a wall-to-wall shower—earth-toned tiles covered walls, floor, and ceiling—with a simple sink and cabinet on one wall and a toilet and urinal on another. A second door led to a small bedroom that was almost more bed than room. The third opened to a room lined with shelves packed to near collapse. It had what she was looking for—the furnace and enough blankets to warm a small army. She increased the temperature from fifty degrees to a balmy seventy, then grabbed a stack of blankets and returned to the couch.

She lay a patched comforter across the brown microsuede, then a soft fleece blanket, before trudging back up the stairs. She shoved her feet back into her boots before heading out the door and down the front stairs to her car. Dax sat up when she popped the hatch, bumping his head on the car's ceiling and leaving a dirty smear on the off-white vinyl.

"Sorry about the mess." He offered an apologetic grimace, reaching up to rub away the spot but stopping when he saw how filthy his hand was. "I've got a buddy who does detailing. I'll hook you up. Everything set in there?"

"Yeah. I cranked up the furnace, found a bunch of blankets," her mouth pulled into a smirk, "drew you a bubble bath, prepared a seven-course 'welcome back to life' meal..."

He'd been nodding along until she got to those last two items. His tired grin flashed white against tanned, dirt-and-blood-smudged skin. "Great. I'm starving."

"Being mostly dead will do that to you. You aren't craving brains or anything, right?"

"Hard to say." Dax sniffed loudly near Zelda's head

as she ducked into the Subaru's cargo space and slid her arms around his chest. "You do smell delicious."

A shiver ran down her spine when his warm breath tickled her scalp. "Keep that up and I'll leave you out here."

Zelda maneuvered him so his legs dangled over the bumper, one on each side of her legs. With a grunt of effort on both their parts, she helped lower him to the ground, trying to ignore how his triceps bunched with the effort or how the muscles of his torso shifted against her.

The only sound was the scraping of the tarp against snow as she dragged it and its occupant the several feet to the open basement window. Dax leaned forward to catch the window casement. Between his pulling and Zelda's pushing, they managed to get him perched on the sill.

"If you head into the basement and guide me down, I can get myself in."

"Sounds like a plan."

Her exhausted legs screamed in protest as she climbed the front stairs, slid off her boots, then descended into the basement. Again. Dax was right where she'd left him, sitting with his arms braced against the window frame and legs dangling over the sill. Zelda climbed onto the couch and found herself standing between his legs, her face level with his.

Dax's eyes met hers. They were pretty—mahogany brown with flecks of gold, framed by thick, dark lashes. He cleared his throat, shaking his head like he was trying to clear it. "If you can just keep my legs from fouling up, I can support my weight. I was the pull-up champ at my gym. Impressive, right?"

"So, how do I...?" Zelda awkwardly wrapped her arms around his thighs. Her hands slipped between them, fingertips settling into the groove along the inner edge of his well-developed quadriceps. Her cheeks heated. "Sorry, I shouldn't... Umm..."

"Huh?" Dax grunted, focused on lowering himself through the window and clearly unable to feel what her hands were doing. But her apology got his attention. His gaze shifted to her furiously blushing face, then dropped to her hands, a slow smile pulling at his lips. "Oh."

When he shot her a wink, Zelda took a hasty step back, her foot slipping off the edge of the couch cushion. Before she realized what she was doing, her grip tightened around Dax's thighs to stop herself from falling. The next few seconds were a blur of flailing limbs and flying blankets and pillows. When calm descended once more, Zelda found herself face-planted into Dax's groin.

"I'd say, 'while you're down there,' but since I can't feel anything, it'd be a wasted effort."

"Well, things seem to be working, whether you feel anything or not," Zelda muttered under her breath as she scrambled to her feet. Her face—make that her whole body—felt like it was going to spontaneously combust. It would be a mercy if it did.

"What?" Dax's gaze dropped to the noticeable bulge in his jeans. It was an area Zelda was trying hard, and failing, not to look at. He frowned, pink tinging his cheeks. "Well, I'll be damned. I can't feel a thing. The damn thing clearly has a mind of its own. I apologize on its behalf."

Oh, but I did, and I'd like to feel it again. "I won't hold it against you." Zelda bit back a groan when Dax chuckled, not sure if she was thankful or disappointed he didn't retort with something lewd like, "But I will."

Focus, girl! She took a deep breath, climbing back up to shut the window before hopping off the couch. "I better rebandage those wounds before I run out of steam. Some are deep and probably need stitches. Do you think your friend has a first-aid kit and a needle and thread somewhere?"

"If he did, it would probably be in the storage room where you got the blankets. You could check his office upstairs too. While you're up there, maybe you could grab me a change of clothes from the closet." When Zelda nodded in response, Dax's cheeks turned a deeper red. "Look, I don't know how to ask this without sounding... umm... Since some things, or functions, seem to be working without me feeling the need to act on them... Well, what if I—"

"No need to say more. I catch your drift." Zelda tried not to look directly at Dax, not wanting to make him feel more self-conscious than he already seemed to. She imagined she'd feel terrible too if she'd no control over her body's basic functions, embarrassed to have a stranger involved. "Do you want me to help you to the bathroom before I go in search of supplies? Or find something that might work as a bedpan of sorts?"

"Fuck if I know." Dax sighed, then raked his fingers through his dark hair, a shower of dirt and twigs hitting the blanket. The corners of his mouth tugged downward, a crease forming between his brows. "What I really want is for you to help me into the shower, turn it on as hot as it will go—"

"Given your injuries, that would be a bad idea."

"I'm covered in dirt, blood, and wolf slobber. The stink is making me want to tear off what's left of my skin. I think it's a great idea."

Something about his words turned her blood cold, but since she wasn't sure what, she shook off the feeling. "I'll see what I can find to get you cleaned up." When Dax started to voice his objections, Zelda interrupted. "If it helps, I played nurse to my grandmother during the last several years of her life. There's not much I haven't seen or dealt with. We're talking *Exorcist*-level shit."

"Great. Comparing me to your grandmother."

Zelda chuckled, the nervous sound grating in her ears. She turned toward the storage room. "There's at least one way you're different."

"Oh yeah, how's that?"

Zelda ducked into the storage room, her hand rising to her face as she thought of what she'd felt pressed against her cheek through the tattered remains of his jeans. In that moment, all she'd wanted was to rub along that hardened ridge like a cat with its favorite catnip toy. But there was no way she could be as bold as to claim *that* as the difference.

"You can't compel spirits to lash out at me if I screw up."

CHAPTER 5

Dax couldn't deny it. There was something almost erotic about a pretty woman focusing all her attention on his body, even if it was only to treat his injuries. Oh, and to give him a sponge bath, apparently. He'd never had any naughty nurse fantasies, but Zelda was filling his head with triple-X-rated ideas.

Zelda had laid a clean tarp, topped with several layers of towels that still smelled of bleach and lavender fabric softener, on the floor next to the couch. Two large, steaming bowls sat on the edge of the tarp with a stack of rags. She'd traded in her jeans and wool sweater for Toby's gym clothes—a pair of nylon running shorts and a Mount Marathon race T-shirt. But his buddy had never looked so good in them.

Kneeling next to Dax, Zelda guided his hand to her lap, settling the back of it into the groove where her bare thighs touched. Careful fingers plucked at bandages that had seen better days. What had probably once been white cloth was now a muted rust color from the mixture of blood and dirt. Their stink could curl nose hairs, and the skin under them itched like he'd rolled in a patch of devil's club. While he wasn't anxious to see the wreckage beneath, he was ready for them to go.

Zelda dipped a rag into one of the bowls, a similar smell as the bandages wafting toward Dax when she squeezed out the excess water. He must have made a face, because she said in a soothing voice, "Maybe it would be better if you didn't look."

"It's fine. Blood doesn't bother me, especially my own."

Zelda's frown told him that she wasn't reassured. "I'd imagine not. But this is different from a bloody nose or a split lip or knuckles."

"I know, but I'd like to see for myself how bad those fucking wolves tore me up. I sank a lot of time and money into my tattoos, only to have those flea-bitten mutts ruin them. And my next one was going to be a wolf. I guess I don't have to bother—they left their mark without me having to go under the needle. Chicks dig scars just as much as tattoos, right?" Dax's half-hearted attempt at humor fell flat, ending with Zelda swallowing hard. "Forget about me. Are you going to be okay?"

"Of course." Zelda's smile seemed forced, an obvious attempt to reassure him. "This isn't the first time I've bandaged you up, although you probably don't remember it. When soul and body reunite, there's usually a loss of memory from that time apart."

"So, when people die and say they remember reliving

their life, going through a tunnel and heading for a bright light...?"

"Do you remember something like that?"

"I don't know." Dax wasn't about to say it to Zelda, since it sounded stupid even to him, but he remembered *something*—light and warmth. It had drawn him in and once he'd given in, embraced him.

But his most vivid memory was of an angel's lips melding with his. Zelda's lips. *Would it feel as blissful if I kissed her now?* Zelda's cheeks reddened when his gaze dropped to her mouth. The pink triangle of her tongue swept across the plushness of her lower lip. *Would it still taste like cider?*

Dax drew in a silent breath, fighting the temptation to sample it for himself. "You promised me a couple things when we were in the woods—a stiff drink and an explanation."

"Yeah, I did."

"I think I could use that drink now."

Zelda nodded, pushing to her feet and heading to the bar. Toby's tiny nylon running shorts showcased the lean lines of her legs and the perky roundness of her ass. But appreciation turned to something more primal when he glimpsed the crease where her thigh met her ass and the lacy edge of fire-engine-red panties.

"What the—" Was he getting a hard-on? He'd heard of phantom limbs, but this? When he'd gotten one earlier, he hadn't felt a damned thing. What was it about this woman, that she could get a rise out of him so easily even when he was dead from the waist down?

"Did you say something?" Zelda called from behind the bar.

"Nothing to worry about." His hand quested downward. *Yup, hard as a rock—definitely not imagining it.* Maybe Zelda was right and the paralysis was just temporary. Who would have thought he'd be thankful for the discomfort of an ill-timed erection?

Although, he doubted Zelda would feel the same. As she popped back up from behind the bar, he snatched a blanket off the couch and pulled it down onto himself. He suddenly had flashbacks to his first girlfriend, a good Catholic girl who he'd traumatized by getting turned on by their fairly chaste kissing, not to mention all those times he'd popped wood in public places and hoped no one had noticed. His awkward teenage moments weren't ones he was keen to relive.

Zelda sauntered back toward him, waving a bottle, seemingly oblivious to his brush with shame. "I think your friend likes whiskey. A stockpile of that and a bottle of rum were all I could find." She set two tumblers on the glass coffee table, then knelt next to his head. "Are you cold?"

"A bit."

"Well, the whiskey will help, as will getting you out of those wet clothes."

"It can wait." Dax fought back a groan as Zelda closed her fingers on the bottom hem of his T-shirt and carefully stripped him of it, tossing the ruined thing toward the edge of the tarp. When she reached for the blanket covering his lower half, he blurted, "Zelda, seriously! I can do it myself."

The fight statistics he'd been reciting to get rid of his hard-on weren't enough, especially with her zeroing in on the fly of his jeans. *God, what is wrong with me?* Just a couple hours before, he'd been dead. That alone should have shut down his libido. But then, sex could be a fanfreaking-tastic way to celebrate life.

He kept a death grip on the blanket with one hand as he worked the button and zipper with the other. Squirming out of wet denim was harder than he thought, especially with one hand and no control over the lower half of his body.

Zelda chewed the inside of her lip for a moment, clearly trying not to watch his struggle. With a sigh, she scooted toward his feet. "I'm sorry. I should have realized... Just because I was raised to think nudity is nothing to be ashamed of, doesn't mean you were. I'm not just trying to get you naked. You really will warm up faster if you get out of these wet things. Let me help. Please. I promise not to look. You can even stay under the blanket."

"I'm not... I can... I don't..." Dax stuttered, every explanation a path to awkward. He took a deep breath, and swallowed back his pride and dignity. "Fine. I'd appreciate some help."

As Zelda pulled off his sneakers, rolled his socks off his feet, and then started to tug his jeans off by pulling on the bottom hem, Dax focused on keeping a grip on the blanket and his boxer briefs. It really wasn't bashfulness. But he'd be damned if the first time he was naked with the woman would be like this, his body a useless wreck.

Dude, seriously! She saved you. She's not just some

groupie, begging for a quick fuck. She's the kind of woman you take your time with, bring home to meet the family.

Zelda gave a small grunt of satisfaction when she finally freed him from his jeans, tossing them toward his T-shirt. She crawled back up toward his head, wiggling her legs beneath his shoulders until her belly bumped against the top of his head. "See! Better, right?"

Oh fuck, not helping. His body fought for control against his brain, nudging him to turn over and nuzzle between her legs. He could smell her over the stinking bandages and bowls of water, her delicate feminine scent storming through him. When she leaned over him to retrieve the glasses of whiskey from the table—her breasts just inches from his face—Dax's cock twitched, like the damned thing was gesturing for her to come closer.

"It moved!"

Oh, God. "I'm sorry."

"Why are you sorry? Thank the Goddess! Look, it moved again!" A smile lit Zelda's face. "And now the other one. We need to celebrate!"

"Other one?"

Zelda's grin faltered as she arched an eyebrow. "Your feet. What did you think...?"

Something in Dax's face must have given him away because her eyes flitted to another part of his anatomy. Her cheeks flushed, the color spreading over her jaw and down her neck to disappear under the T-shirt.

Her teeth worried her lower lip, eyes pinned to the center of his chest as she handed him a glass. "Umm... Well, that's... Drink up and we'll get back to business."

Shit. Way to ruin things for me, buddy. Dax downed

his whiskey in one gulp, then handed the tumbler back to Zelda, who was slamming back her own drink. She scooted out from under his head, set the glasses on the table, and moved to kneel at his side. That time, she didn't put his hand in her lap. Instead, she left it at his side and returned to removing his bandages.

He closed his eyes, trying not to think about the gentle movements of her fingers. *Forget about it, Dax. She's clearly not interested in anything but playing nurse, and not the naughty kind.* Instead of beating himself up for something completely out of his control, he turned his thoughts to what had brought him there—one bad choice after another.

It was hard to believe that just the day before, he'd been heading to Isadora Kane's office to sign papers and weigh in for his fight. And less than a dozen hours later, a return trip to that office had led to his death. Guilt surged as he thought of the woman he'd left behind there. He hoped she was all right.

Now that he was someplace safe, and with a phone, he could call the cops to report what happened. But what could he tell them? A hogtied hostage, Russian mobsters, trained killer wolves, resurrection from the dead. They'd think he was a nutjob.

When Zelda gasped, his eyes flew open. "What?"

She didn't answer, her gaze pinned to his arm for a moment before she tore into the bandages on his chest, then the ones on his other arm, like a kid with a Christmas present. When she flicked back the blanket and started on the bandage around his thigh, her raised ass wiggling and red panties flashing at him like a fly in front of a trout, he knew he had to put a stop to it before he did something reckless. Or perverted. His fingers twitched with the need to wrap around her hips and drag her back so he could sink his teeth into a rounded cheek.

Horndog. The word popped into his head in his adoptive mother, Carmen's, voice. She'd called him that when she'd caught him putting the moves on his high school math tutor instead of studying. And just like then, it sounded more exasperated than angry.

Zelda's insistent fingers stripping him of his bandages and exploring his skin was taking that desperate, awkward teenage horniness and dialing it up to eleven. Dax caught hold of her hands. "Damn it, Zelda, what is it?"

"See for yourself." Zelda pulled free, sweeping a hand over his body like a gameshow host, announcing, "And look what you've won."

Dax steeled himself as he raised an arm in front of his face, memories from the night before chasing through his thoughts. He could still feel the searing pain of wolf teeth and claws, still see the shredded flesh. That wasn't what he saw now. Instead, he saw scabbed wounds, well on their way to healing, crisscrossing the tattooed skin.

Pushing himself up until he was sitting, he ignored the slight dizziness that came with the movement. He sent questing hands over his arms, down his chest, and over his thigh. They confirmed what his eyes told him— the wounds' edges were knitting neatly together.

How is that possible?

Zelda took advantage of his upright position to peel the bandages from his back. Her hand was warm when it ran over the skin there, the pads of her fingertips tracing parallel lines.

"What did you put on those bandages?" Dax pivoted to look at Zelda.

Her eyes widened as she shook her head. "Nothing that would have healed you so quickly."

"So, what did?"

Zelda nibbled at her lip as she returned to exploring the healing wounds, occasionally leaning in to look more closely. His heart stuttered every time he felt her warm breath on his skin. The ache between his legs returned, uncomfortable enough to elicit a groan. "Zelda..."

He wasn't expecting her to lunge toward him, but she did, stopping with her face just inches from his. The thought of gripping her silky blonde hair and dragging her closer struck him dumb.

As if she knew what he was thinking, her gaze dropped to his mouth. But instead of closing the distance between them, her fingertips slipped between his lips, raising them so she could look at his teeth.

"Christ, woman, what are you doing?" Dax reared back.

Zelda sat back on her haunches, her eyes turning to the empty glasses on the table. "It's probably time for me to keep my other promise—an explanation. There's no easy way to say this, so I'm just going to dive right in. I was hoping..." A frown furrowed her brow as she shook her head. "I mean, you were dead, or mostly so. That should have... See, death is kind of like hitting a reset button when it comes to curses and other magic. But I think in your case, for some reason..."

So much for diving right in. Dax fought back the urge to shake her. "What?"

"You're... Well, you've been infected with the werewolf curse."

"Werewolves? Come on! You're fucking with me! Right?" Dax's eyes searched hers, clearly looking for any hint that she was kidding.

"You can handle the idea of me bringing you back from the dead, but werewolves are unbelievable?"

"Well, I... Werewolves?" Dax stared down at his hands, flexing his fingers. "You mean rip out of their skin and grow hair and fangs at the full moon, kill everything in sight monsters? Like *An American Werewolf in London* or something? Seriously?"

Dax shook his head roughly, his fingers threading into his hair and tightening into fists. He seemed more confused than angry. But if the curse had reached the point of rapid healing, perhaps he wasn't far from turning. And without an alpha to control him...

Zelda scooted until her back hit the couch, then tucked her legs under her in case she needed to make a run for it. Not that she'd ever be quick enough to escape a werewolf. "I'd never joke about something like that. I know it sounds crazy, but it's true. The beasts that attacked you are werewolves. They work for Isadora Kane, the woman who recruited you to fight last night."

"Huge Russian guys?"

"You've met Yuri and Dimitri?"

"Yeah. More than once, apparently." Dax pulled the bandage from his throat and ran his hand over it. His Adam's apple bobbed. "After I found the woman, Ms. Kane ordered them to get rid of me."

Zelda's heart stopped in her chest. "There was a woman?"

"Yeah. A pretty little blonde. I thought Ms. Kane was kidding when she called the woman her hostage. She was —" Dax stopped speaking and peered at Zelda, his eyes narrowing. "She looked a bit like you, actually."

"My sister." Zelda nodded. "Isadora was serious. Larissa really is her prisoner."

"What the hell?" Dax's brow furrowed, his body tensing like he was about to leap to his feet. "Have you gone to the cops?"

"A couple are supernaturals and on her payroll. So, no." Before she knew what she was doing, Zelda was back at Dax's side, clinging to his hands. His scabbed knuckles felt rough against her palms. "My sister... Was she all right?"

Dax stared down at their joined hands, not meeting her gaze. "She didn't seem... Well, I wasn't sure what I'd walked into. But she didn't look hurt, just unhappy with her...circumstances." Patches of red appeared along his jaw, the muscle there twitching like he was upset.

"What aren't you telling me?"

"I was going to get her out of there, but Ms. Kane and her goons showed up before I could. I'm sorry, Zelda."

"Where?"

"Mabon Enterprises' office. In a building downtown, corner of Third and G."

"Third floor?" When Dax nodded, Zelda leaped to her feet. "I've got to go. If I'm not back in four hours, call the Chocolate Lounge and ask for Lucy. Tell her—"

"Hold on!" Dax caught her ankle, his grip tight enough that she couldn't easily pull free. "I doubt your sister is still there. It didn't look like she'd been there long. And since I saw her, they probably moved her."

"They probably think you're dead, so they wouldn't need to worry about you telling the police or anyone else." And if they didn't think he was dead, they'd know he was infected and could be made loyal to the pack if they found him before First Turn.

Zelda dropped to the couch, pressing her fingers against her eyes and rubbing until she saw stars. Goddess, she was tired. Worn down to her very soul. And even that felt drained.

She freed a heavy sigh. Apparently, her common sense was zapped as well. She didn't need to go in person to see if Larissa was still at Isadora's office. There were others who could do it for her.

Using the barest touch of will, Zelda silently called for Billie, plucking at their connection like she was tuning a guitar. It took a few minutes, but the spirit popped in, perching next to Zelda on the couch.

She offered a tired smile in greeting. "How are things at Coven House, Billie?"

The woman started to answer, but Dax interrupted. "Billie?"

Zelda waved a hand toward the spirit. "She's one of my oldest friends, a ghost. Billie, you remember Dax from Eklutna Lake."

"Of course." Billie offered a matter-of-fact nod as her gaze swept over Dax. "He is a werewolf."

"Yeah, I know. I'm such an idiot. I should have realized it sooner." Zelda could sense Dax's growing discomfort. It was like that with everyone. Eventually, they caught her talking to a spirit, got weirded out, and then avoided her like she had a virulent case of death.

It wasn't likely to do much good, but she offered him a reassuring smile anyway. "Sorry. Billie just made the brilliant observation that you're a werewolf. Just pretend I'm a crazy woman babbling to herself. I'll fill you in after." Zelda sighed when Dax shook his head with a bemused frown. "Billie, can you go to Mabon Enterprises' downtown office and check if Larissa is there?"

The spirit smoothed a hand over her transparent curls. "I will try, but the high priestess has been warding her spaces against spirits since enlisting you in her schemes."

"As much as I wish otherwise, Isadora isn't an idiot."

"No. But she is furious."

"And a total bitch."

Billie gave Zelda a stern look that had more to do with her foul language than any loyalty to the high priestess. "Isadora has been interrogating your coven sisters about your lover, trying to find you. Perhaps you should telephone her."

"And tell her what? That I'm taking a couple days off to shag my boyfriend." Zelda swallowed hard, shrinking under the weight of Dax's unspoken question. "My imaginary one."

"I assumed you would not want to abandon your sisters to Isadora's wrath." The vibration of Billie's energy shifted with her frown. "Was I wrong?"

Zelda treaded dangerous ground. The spirit wasn't just loyal to her but to the entire coven, clinging to the vows spoken during her invocation even after death. Zelda's throat tightened. She could take a lesson in loyalty and duty from the spirit.

"I'm sorry. You're right. I'll try to think of something to get Isadora off the others' backs." Zelda spoke in her most soothing voice, opening her inner wards just enough so the spirit could feel she was sincere but not glimpse her actual thoughts. If Zelda had her way, anything she planned would permanently free her, Larissa, and the coven from Isadora. When Billie nodded in acceptance, Zelda continued, "Please check Mabon's offices, and if you see no sign of Larissa, tail the Russians. Come back to me as soon as you find anything."

"As you wish." With a bow of her head, Billie vanished.

"Sorry about that." Zelda was finding it hard to meet Dax's stare. The last thing she wanted to see there was confirmation that he thought she was crazy.

"Witches, covens, werewolves, ghosts." He shook his head slowly, a frown furrowing his brow. "So, the woman who hired me to fight is the high priestess of a coven. The woman I tried to save, who I pointlessly died for, is your sister. The guys who did it are Russian werewolves who work for Ms. Kane. You can raise and talk to the dead. I'm now a werewolf. Does that cover it? Anything else I need to know?"

"How much time do you have?" Zelda felt a corner of her mouth curl upward.

"Until the next full moon, apparently," Dax sighed. One thing was clear—he'd been paying attention. Clearly, he was smarter than the average muscle head.

"The wonderful world of the supernatural is out there, just waiting for you to discover it," Zelda said in her best movie trailer narrator voice. "Look, I'll fill you in as best I can, but a full info dump will take time we don't really have. For now, the most important thing you need to know is that the local pack, not to mention the coven, bows to High Priestess Isadora. Or as she thinks of herself, Queen Goddess on High, Most Beautiful and Alluring of Creatures."

"Great." Dax flopped back to the floor, dragging his hands over his hair. "And this egomaniac wants me dead and has an army of witches and wolves to do it."

"None in my coven are killers. We live by the Rule of Three—anything you do, the energy you send out into the world, will be returned threefold." *What will resurrecting Dax bring back to me?* "But the pack doesn't follow that rule. They do Isadora's dirty work." Zelda tried to keep the scorn out of her voice. After all, Dax was now part of Bold Peak Pack. According to pack law, those bitten were the responsibility of the biter.

According to Council agreement, she should return Dax to the pack. But... what if she didn't? Having a werewolf on her side could even the odds. Not that she intended to hold him, or enlist his help, against his will. "The pack might think you're dead, but I wouldn't put it past them to come back and check. Werewolves are notoriously hard to kill, almost as bad as vampires, and you're—"

"Vampires are real?" Dax exclaimed, rising to his elbows. "Sure, why not. Next, you'll be telling me there are sasquatches, dragons, aliens—"

"I can't speak to aliens, but—"

"Oh, God. You're really serious. You really think I'm a werewolf."

"We won't know for sure until you turn, but the rapid healing of your wounds is a definite sign."

His desolate expression left her wanting to hug him, to offer some sort of comfort. She could imagine how alone he felt. When her parents had first realized Zelda's affinity for the dead, they'd dropped the bomb that she was an abomination and her mother had fled. Zelda had been incapable of even accepting Billie's comforting, too angry at the ghost for bringing their rejection upon her, destroying her life. It had taken some time for her to stop blaming the spirit.

Would Dax blame her the same way?

"It's not all bad news." Zelda offered what she hoped looked like a cheerful smile. "At this rate, you'll hardly have scars by sundown. It's a perk of the curse. I've seen werewolves who were beaten nearly to death be completely healed within hours." There was no need to tell him those beatings were usually pack inflicted. "Your opponent from last night, Hunter, didn't have a bruise on him by the time we sat down for feast."

"He's a werewolf?"

"The participants in Isadora's fights are almost always supernatural, mostly shifters of some sort."

"How did I—"

"Win? Good question. I'm guessing a lot of people lost money on your fight. You were the clear underdog. Ha! Get it?" She'd hoped to at least get a chuckle out of Dax, but he remained silent. "I think it was a combination of you catching him by surprise, being a good fighter, and being very lucky."

"I don't know about lucky."

Zelda folded her hands in her lap, her fingers knotting and twisting in an effort not to reach for him. "I know it doesn't seem like it now, but hopefully someday you'll see how wrong you are. To win a fight against a werewolf, to be brought back from death..."

"Maybe. I'm still hoping I'll go to sleep and wake up in my bed, realize this has all just been some weird dream."

Dax pressed a hand against his mouth to stifle a yawn. He scooted toward the couch, reaching back and gripping the cushions. When he started dragging himself onto it, Zelda rose to help, but he waved her off. After a couple minutes of bunching muscles and quiet cursing, he managed to maneuver himself next to her.

"So, you're a witch. Can the others in your coven do what you do? Ms. Kane?"

"You mean raise the dead, talk to spirits?" She waited for his nod before continuing. "No, my skills are... specialized. Few of my kind have an affinity for the dead. The coven, as well as the Grand Coven and Council—a kind of United Nations of supernatural entities that governs us—carefully watches the ones who do. At one time, Council Enforcers exterminated those like me.

Necromancers attract spirits, but they're drawn to them as well. And not all are friendly—spirit or necromancer, I guess."

"And your sister?"

"Is not like me. She's innocent, good. I..." Zelda dropped her gaze to her hands in her lap, trying to keep the desperation from her voice. "I'd do anything to get her back, pay any cost." When Dax's hand covered hers, giving a reassuring squeeze, she took a deep breath. "I was hoping you'd help me, help her."

"By help, you mean?"

"Storm the castle, defeat the wicked witch and her werewolves, rescue the damsel. The usual hero stuff."

"Oh." The sound hung in the air between them for a moment.

"Like I said, I'd be willing to pay any price you name..."

He cleared his throat as he released her hands. "This has been a lot to take in. I need some time."

"I understand," Zelda replied, trying not to let her disappointment show in her voice or on her face.

"Is being brought back from the dead like having a concussion? Do I need to be kept awake, watched?"

"No, your spirit should be firmly lodged in your body. Unless someone kills you again, that is."

Dax's jaw cracked with his next face-splitting yawn. "I think I need sleep. Dying sure takes a lot out of you."

"As does resurrection," Zelda said under her breath.

"I'd imagine so." Dax turned and slid back until he wedged himself into a corner of the couch. He stretched his legs out, his feet nearly touching Zelda's thigh. Taking the blanket she offered with a nod of thanks, he spread it over himself. "Can you close the blinds and turn off the lights?"

"Yeah. Of course." Zelda fought back a sigh.

She climbed up to close the blinds, taking care not to step on Dax's legs. Once she slid off the couch, she moved around the room to shut the blinds on the other windows. By the time she reached the light switch at the base of the stairs and flicked it off, she was ready to curl into a ball right there on the floor. She hadn't thought about their sleeping arrangements. Maybe she could just curl up in the guest bedroom.

"Zelda," Dax quietly called. His voice slurred a bit when he spoke. "Plenty of room here on the couch. I'd appreciate the company, if you don't mind."

Zelda swallowed hard as she nodded, then realized he probably couldn't see it. Or maybe he could. She'd no idea how good a fledgling werewolf could see in the dark. She returned to the couch and grabbed a blanket, curling into the opposite corner from Dax.

After a few moments of quiet breathing, he said, "Gotta be honest. I'm no hero."

"I'm not *really* looking for one. Just someone to watch my back, kick some ass if needed, and stay out of my way while I do whatever it takes to help my sister."

Dax was silent for a moment, the only sound his slow, even breaths. Zelda wished she could see him. Convinced he'd fallen asleep, she nearly jumped when his deep voice sounded from the darkness. "Let's talk some more about it after a few hours of sleep, okay?"

She released the breath she'd apparently been

holding. He wasn't saying no. Hope eased the weight that had been settling on her chest. "Okay. Sweet dreams, Dax."

"G'night, Zelda." Dax's chuckle was as soft as his whisper. "Don't let the werewolves bite."

CHAPTER 6

ZELDA WASN'T SURE WHAT WOKE HER—THE SMELL OF coffee or the sounds of the shower, bluesy music, and slightly off-tune but enthusiastic singing. She opened her eyes to a dark room, the only light coming from beneath the bathroom door. There was no sign of sunlight seeping through the window blinds.

She sighed. An entire day lost. Well, at the very least, it was after three thirty in the afternoon, when the sun set. Why hadn't Billie returned with news of Larissa or what was going on at Coven House yet?

Once she fought free of the lure of warm blankets, Zelda slid out of her cozy burrow, flipped on the light, and padded over to her backpack. It took her a few minutes to find her cell phone in the jumble of hastily repacked ritual supplies. The display told her that it was later than she thought—nearly eight o'clock—and that the battery was nearly dead. Not that it mattered. The device was little more than a useless hunk of plastic and circuitry. No signal.

Shit... She really needed to check in with Isadora, but how? The retro-style pay telephone mounted on the wood-paneled wall next to the bar caught her eye. It would be risky to call the woman or Coven House from that. The number could show up on caller ID, and someone could match it to an address. It would be safer to leave the house and find a place where she could get a cell signal. Or...

She took a deep breath as she picked up the corded receiver and dialed Lucy's number. The line rang four times, each one tightening the band around her chest another notch. She nearly cried out with joy when Lucy answered.

Lucy's shouted "Hello?" was barely audible over the loud techno music in the background.

The thumping bass echoed in Zelda's chest. "Lucy, it's me. Are you all right? Everyone else?" For a moment, all she could hear was a muffled remix, like the woman had shoved the phone into her pocket.

There was an odd echo, but the music was quieter, when Lucy whispered, "Where are you? Your phone keeps going right to voice mail. Isadora's flipping out trying to find you."

"Long story. You alone?"

"For now. I'm in the bathroom at 'Koots, so that could change any minute. Seriously, where are you?"

Zelda released a relieved breath. Lucy being at her favorite hook-up bar meant Isadora hadn't locked down the coven. Or maybe she was hoping Lucy would lead her to Zelda. *Ah... paranoia... 'tis a wonderful thing.*

"It's better if you don't know specifics. I'm helping a friend through a death, and will be out of touch for a bit since there's no cell coverage where I'm staying. Can you pass that on to Isadora? Let her know I'll be back in a couple days?"

"Yeah, I suppose. Or I could just let her keep thinking you're off getting your groove back. That'd be more fun. Oh, just so we have our stories straight, your guy is a barista named Richard. He wooed you with free skinny mochas, his IT skills, and his huge package."

"Flaming hells! Now Isadora will have her wolves searching every coffee shop and shack in town. What if they actually find a guy with that name, hurt him to find me?"

"You worry too much. Even if Isadora sent the wolves hunting, there's a thousand coffee spots in the Anchorage Bowl. It'll take them days. And they wouldn't hurt anyone unless..." Lucy sucked in a noisy breath. "Shit! You're not doing anything stupid that would piss her off, like trying to rescue Larissa, are you?"

"I'm helping a friend, like I said." *Not entirely a lie.*

"Like you have any outside the coven except... This is a dead 'friend,' isn't it?"

"No." *Not anymore, at least.* Zelda glanced toward the bathroom, where Dax was singing along with the song's chorus. For a heartbeat, she considered telling Lucy who her 'friend' was. The witch would be beyond jealous. *Yeah...not the best idea, pissing off one of my few allies.* "Please, just tell Isadora something so she doesn't think I've abandoned Larissa and the coven. I'm almost afraid to ask, but what has she been saying?"

"Not a peep about Larissa. But she's had plenty to say about you, bitching about how you're selfish, unreliable, spiteful, ungrateful. You're not her favorite person." A toilet flushed in the background on Lucy's end. "Where are you? A karaoke bar? Someone needs to tell that guy to stop butchering Hozier like that."

"I think he's pretty good." Zelda fought back a smile as she imagined Dax wet and naked, his shampoo mohawk flopping as he sang into a handheld showerhead about kissing "like real people do." Oh, what she wouldn't give to be his audience of one for a shower concert. She could play groupie, offer to scrub his back, or other parts. Heat flooded her cheeks, not to mention other parts.

"Look, I've got to run. Take care of yourself and the others. And please delete this call from your phone log, okay? This isn't where I'm staying. I'm just borrowing the poor guy's phone to check in." Zelda hated lying to her coven sister, but it was best for everyone. "No need to risk siccing Isadora or her wolves on him. I'll be home as soon as I can."

"Will do. But what if I need to get ahold of you?"

"Leave a message on my voice mail. I'll try to check it regularly."

"Okay. Good luck with your friend."

Yeah, like luck is ever on my side. "Thanks. Good luck with Isadora."

Zelda hung up the phone, immediately dialing out again to check her voice mail. Surprisingly, there were no messages. She returned the receiver to its cradle and collapsed onto the bar stool below it. There was no way Isadora's silence was a good thing. The woman had to be up to something, but what? The dearth of threats terrified Zelda more than her usual intimidations.

The unexpected rattle of the bathroom door opening sent her heart skipping. Or maybe it was Dax's entrance. He wore nothing but a pair of red flannel pajama pants—covered with Santa-hatted dancing polar bears—slung low on his hips. The tanned and tattooed expanse of his muscular chest was on full display, the chiseled lines of his abs and Adonis belt luring her gaze downward.

"Hey, you're up. I thought I heard your voice. I made coffee if you want some."

"Thanks," Zelda mumbled, struggling to raise her eyes to meet his instead of ogling him—a fight she wasn't likely to win. *But I've got a valid reason for looking, right? Completely clinical.* "I'm so happy to see you walking."

"You and me both." He showed off with a bit of shadow boxing before sliding in next to her at the bar.

She returned his grin, pressing her hands between her thighs to keep from reaching toward his unmarred skin. Despite a valid reason to touch him, she suspected that once she started, she wouldn't be able to stop. "Your wounds look mostly healed. How do you feel?"

Dax's muscles rippled as he stretched across the bar top in front of her, flipping over a pair of mugs sitting next to the coffee maker and filling them. "Like I could run a marathon up and down a mountain." He slid a mug in front of her before tugging the sleeve of her borrowed Mount Marathon T-shirt.

"Look…" The playful gesture took a more serious turn as he cupped her shoulder. "I wanted to thank you."

The guilt Zelda carried turned into a cold ball in her belly. It wasn't like his resurrection was a selfless gesture that deserved thanks. And if he helped in her attempt to rescue Larissa, it could be temporary. "You don't—"

Dax gripped her shoulders and turned her to face him, the swiveling seat offering an assist. "You found me, patched me up, brought me back to life. I owe you more than I could ever repay."

"Really, you don't—"

"Damn it!" He gave her a little shake. "Will you just say, 'you're welcome'?"

Zelda sucked in a breath, her lungs filling with his warm natural scent, nearly hidden under Irish Spring soap and mint toothpaste. *How long before he starts to stink of wolf? The next full moon? Sooner?*

"Fine. I'll say it if it means you let go." She couldn't stop herself from breathing him in again. "You're welcome. Happy?"

"Close enough." The way he looked at her left her thinking he wasn't just talking about her giving in to his demand. He cocked his head as he scrutinized her for a moment, the silence dragging on. "You look so familiar."

"Of course I do," Zelda chuckled, a nervous sound dangerously close to being a giggle. "I'd be worried that you suffered brain damage if I didn't." She wiggled free from his grip and turned to retrieve her coffee, hoping to break away from the intensity of his dark-eyed stare.

"No, I mean from before this morning. Wait… Have we—"

"Met?" Zelda surveyed the bar top for something that might hold sugar, but didn't see anything. "Besides up at the lake? Yeah."

"Oh?" He trailed his gaze down Zelda's body and then back up, pausing at her mouth. "I knew it. So, we've —" He arched an eyebrow suggestively.

"Ha! No." Zelda feigned nonchalance even as her stomach flip-flopped. "Good to know you think we might have hooked up and you don't remember it. I'm not sure if that says more about you or what you think about me." She sat back on the stool and crossed an arm over her chest. "We met after your fight last night. You dismissed me like pureed liver on a Triscuit at Costco sample day."

She raised the mug to her lips, nearly spitting the foul liquid out the moment it assaulted her tongue. Her voice seemed to pay the price for her decision to swallow it down. "Which reminds me," she coughed as she pushed the cup away, "I didn't get a chance to say it earlier, but congratulations on winning your fight last night. The look on Isadora's face when you blew her off will bring me joy for years to come. There you go. Debt paid."

"Seriously? That can't be right. Why don't I remember?"

"It was right after your fight. Your brother Jamie introduced you to Lucy and me."

Dax scratched at his jaw, his expression going slack. After a moment, he shook his head, a grin spreading across his face. "Blonde Bimbo Barbie!"

Zelda felt something inside her sink. She tightened her arm around herself before hitting him with a scowl. "Glad you remember."

His eyes widened. "No, I meant your friend, not you. I didn't even notice you."

"Gee, thanks."

"Fuck, I'm bad at this." Dax dragged his fingers through his dark hair as he noisily exhaled. "I'm sorry. Let me explain."

"Can't wait."

"My brother is always introducing me to girls, but he's got terrible taste. Every one's been nothing but trouble, so now I avoid his setups like a kick to the nuts. I guess the joke's on me this time."

"What do you mean?"

Dax's grin sent a rush of warmth southward. "If I'd gone home with you, maybe I wouldn't have ended up in a shallow grave."

Gone home with us? A bit presumptuous there, buddy. But then, maybe he'd read Lucy, the one-night-stand queen, pretty well. If Zelda had a dollar for every boy toy that she'd shooed out of Coven House once Lucy lost interest... "Things still would have been awkward and uncomfortable in the morning."

"I doubt that. But at least there would have been less dirt and blood."

"Maybe not."

Dax again offered a suggestive arch of his eyebrow as he inched towards Zelda. "Well, now I'm definitely intrigued."

"I'll be sure to pass that on to Lucy." Zelda rolled her eyes. "Just a word of warning, she'll probably want to 'punish' you for rejecting her—"

"She's not the one who interests me." Dax leaned closer.

"But I thought..." Zelda's heart stuttered when he tucked a strand of hair behind her ear.

Dax brushed his fingertips along its outer curve, toying with the row of small silver hoops. Strong fingers curled around the nape of her neck as he drew her closer. Warm brown eyes searched hers, holding her gaze as he brushed the tip of his thumb over her lips.

"Thought wrong, angel."

Goddess, is he going to...?

He closed the scant distance between them, warm lips grazing hers, testing, questioning. She must have given the answer he was looking for because the corners of his eyes crinkled, his mouth curving into a grin against hers.

His lips brushed hers, his whisper husky, as he pointed out, "You didn't close your eyes."

"Neither did you. Is that—"

The press of his mouth interrupted her, taking advantage of her parted lips. The tip of his tongue flicked against hers, testing again. "You taste like coffee."

"Hope it tastes better on me than it did in the cup."

His chuckle vibrated under her hands, pressed against the silky skin of his chest. Nudging her knees apart with his hips, he stepped in as close as the stool would allow. He cupped her face with warm hands, his eyes searching hers. "You okay with this?"

She nodded so quickly—her body taking control since her brain was incapable of thinking anything other than 'kiss me'—it almost gave her whiplash. As if he could hear her thoughts, his lips returned to teasing hers, luring her to the edge of the seat, closer to the hard heat of his body.

No one had ever kissed her like this—equal parts play, exploration, and seduction. It was like he was committing every sigh and moan to memory, taking his time to understand what she liked. Not that there was anything she didn't. The man's mouth was magic.

Her mind filled with fantasies of blissful hours of kisses, touches, lovemaking. But it was fickle, also raising the alarm—*stop before things go too far. Disaster always follows when I let anyone too close. No good will come from it.*

Her body, however, completely disagreed—*we want closer, and the 'fabulously good' that will follow if his kissing skills are any indication.*

Zelda was inclined to side with her body. Besides, it would be damn near impossible to put distance between them now that she'd had a taste of him. It would be like wandering parched out of the desert, being handed a canteen filled with cool water, and drinking only a sip before tossing it aside to empty onto the sand.

Somehow her brain wrestled back control for a moment, and she whispered, "Maybe we shouldn't. Nightingale syndrome. Transference." But it seemed unwilling to admit, let alone speak, the real reason.

"Desire." The soul-deep rumble of his one-word rebuttal drew her back in.

His lips were gentle, sending shivers of pleasure through her at each touch. There were no demands, just an almost languid build toward a seemingly inevitable goal. If he'd taken a more aggressive approach, it would have been easier to push him away, but this? It was as if he knew she needed him to take it slow.

Goddess, help me... I need to tell him the truth before he kisses me completely stupid. If he still wants me then... The words rushed out on a shuddering breath. "It's the resurrection. When I brought you back, I bound your spirit to mine. Just temporarily, I thought, but..."

Instead of stepping away at her confession, he rested his forehead against hers. His fingers drifted down her neck, his palm settling over her heart. "What does that mean?"

Her mind blanked except to silently wish Dax's hand would slip just a little lower. As if in answer to her prayer it did, his mouth languidly kissing its way downward. Without a thought, her head tipped back to give him better access.

"What does that mean, Zelda?" Dax repeated, the words hot against the crook of her neck.

Zelda released the breath she'd been holding, fighting to form words. "Worst-case, that I've enslaved your will to my own."

The thought of Dax becoming like Franklin, the only other spirit she'd bound to herself, left her cold. But from what she now understood, the ghost had always been a twisted bastard. If only she'd realized just how evil he was before binding him to her.

No, Dax isn't like him. I'm sure of it.

"Oh, is that all?" Dax nibbled his way along her collarbone to her shoulder and then back again. His thumb circled a nipple that was practically hard enough to cut through her T-shirt. "Other than being more turned on than I've ever been in my life, I don't feel any different. How would we know if we were dealing with this 'worst-case'?"

"Besides you not noticing me the first time we met but now suddenly wanting me?"

"I already explained that. Under the circumstances, you could have been an actual angel—glowing and naked with enormous wings—and I wouldn't have noticed."

"I doubt that." Zelda took a deep breath, steeling herself. "There's a way to prove it. Slap me."

"What?" Dax's head jerked upward and his eyes widened like she'd struck him.

Zelda search out the threads that bound their souls together, grasping them as she tapped into the fury she felt toward Isadora, her parents, the Fates who seemed to delight in tormenting her. She had to be brutal, to mean it. "Slap. Me."

Dax's jaw clenched, his fingers tightening. Zelda could feel his spirit fighting, like a king salmon on the end of a line. She kept up the tension, slowly increasing it. Her own ears rang with it, her head pounding. After a few moments—ones that felt like an eternity—his resistance snapped, the line going slack. His muscles tightened, eyes closing as his hands fell away from her. The thought that she'd broken him left her so hollow she couldn't even bring herself to cringe in anticipation of his slap, just close her eyes. She was an abomination, deserving of it and more.

But instead of striking her, he cupped her face again, his touch firm but gentle. "Zelda, look at me." When she did as he bid, his lips tugged up at the corners. "So, what's the best-case?"

Tears burned hot behind her eyes. He'd resisted. The only way he could have done that was if his will was his own. *But how?* "I don't know. The link between us is there. I feel it."

"I do too." He leaned in, his lips hovering a hair's breadth from hers. "Let's find out."

Zelda's heart thudded at Dax's earnestness. *This is insane.* She'd only known him for twenty-four hours. She shouldn't already feel things for him. And unless she was completely misreading him, he was feeling something for her. It was the resurrection, their spiritual connection. It had to be. Nothing else made sense.

She swallowed hard, like that could lock her heart into its cage, keep it from flying free. "What if this is just the spiritual link drawing us together? You only wanting me because I want you?"

"Does it matter? Want is want. We haven't known each other long—and yeah, maybe you bringing me back from the mostly dead has something to do with it—but that doesn't change that I'm kind of crazy about you." His fingertips traced gently over her lips. "I have been since you kissed me at the lake. But if you don't feel the same..."

Zelda bit her lip, a futile attempt to hold back the truth. But his gaze was relentless, peering deep, drawing it forth. Perhaps she'd lost *her* will to *Dax*. "I've wanted you since I first saw you, at the fights." She took a deep breath. "I'm kind of crazy about you too. Goddess, this is insane!"

The small smile that pulled at his mouth almost

looked relieved, and he freed a breath that fluttered against her face. "So, what are we—"

She interrupted him with a kiss, one that quickly grew from gentle to something more urgent, hungry. His hands teased along the outside edge of her breasts and over her ribs, continuing along the curves of her waist and hips before skimming the bare skin of her thighs. Fingers hooked behind her knees, pulling them toward his waist. When she wrapped her legs around him, his mouth smiled against hers as if she'd done just what he wanted. His hands slid back up her thighs to grip her hips, pulling her even tighter to him.

Zelda slid her hands down the length of his chest, delighting in the smooth heat of his skin, the hard strength beneath it. When she slipped them under the elastic waistband of his pajama pants, Dax groaned. His ass flexed under her grasp as he ground against her. The press of his hardening length between her legs was enough to shatter any thoughts except one: *I want him.*

"Too many clothes." Zelda hooked her thumbs into the back of his waistband and shoved downward.

Dax sucked in a pained breath. "Wait. Caught." His hand squeezed in between them, untangling his erection from the waistband so she could continue to push the pants down.

But he didn't give her any time to sit back and appreciate the view, instead grabbing the hem of her shirt and dragging it over her head. His grin as his gaze lingered on her bared breasts reminded her of a pup being offered his favorite treat.

"So pretty," he whispered as the small pale mounds

disappeared under his tan hands, his palms barely brushing her hardened nipples, teasing.

As he bowed his dark head to kiss one pink tip, then the other, he slid his hands down her torso and over her hips until he cupped her ass. Every inch of her tingled, begging for his touch. His breath was hot against her ear when he asked, "This good for you? Or the couch?"

Words were almost more than she could manage. There was so much more she'd rather be doing with her mouth. She twitched her head toward the couch before diving back in for more kisses.

Again, he grinned against her, apparently pleased with her answer. When he lifted her from the stool, she tightened her limbs around him, pressing herself as close to him as she could get. The friction of skin against skin was delicious, a promise of greater pleasure to come.

His muscles shifted and bunched against her as he turned toward the couch. He supported much of her weight with one hand under her ass—cupping, caressing, fingertips moving tantalizingly close to her sex. The other hand tangled in her hair, his grip keeping her mouth from straying too far from his. After a couple shuffling steps, he kicked free of his pants.

Sweet Goddess, this is really happening. Dax is naked.

As heavenly as he felt, there were a few problems with clinging to him. First, *she* wasn't naked. Second, she still hadn't gotten a good look at him in all his nude glory, although she suspected that she wouldn't be disappointed given what she'd seen and felt pressed against her so far. Third, she didn't want to wait until the couch to feel him inside her. She wanted him now.

But before she could drag him to the floor or suggest they just find a sturdy wall, Dax reached their destination. He lowered them to the couch, sinking into the remnant warmth of her blanket nest. "If I'm going to get you naked—and I *really* need to—you'll have to let go." When she hesitated, not about the nudity but the letting go part, he added, "I promise to make it up to you."

His sultry grin was a fine reward for her compliance, but she wanted more. Her hands smoothed over his shoulders and chest as her feet slid over his ass and down the backs of his thighs, hooking behind them. She could have spent hours—days, weeks, forever—exploring him if it weren't for the urgent need to have him inside her.

Dax's gaze and hands were as greedy as hers, devouring every bare inch of her, from the top of her head to the waistband of her shorts. Yet, he suddenly switched gears—taking his time, sliding his fingertips under the elastic, trailing from one hip bone to the other, drawing them down a bit with each pass.

Zelda tamped down her need, trying to enjoy the slow tease, to focus on appreciating the fine male creature poised between her legs. If he was aware of her watching him, he didn't show it, instead fixated on the sensitive skin he was slowly revealing with each pass of his finger. His desire for her was obvious, perfect white teeth catching at his full lower lip and his cock standing at full attention.

When his fingertip finally brushed over her pelvic bone, she groaned, "Goddess... Enough teasing." Grabbing the elastic waistband of her shorts and panties,

Zelda yanked them off, nearly kicking Dax in the chin in her haste.

"Sorry." She shot him a sheepish grin. Was it possible to get drunk off a person? She tapped a toe against his square chin before trailing her feet down his chest and over his belly, sliding one along his hardened length before planting her feet on either side of his thighs and shamelessly letting her knees part.

This wasn't like her. She'd always been more of a go-along-for-the-ride, do-it-silently-in-the-dark kind of girl. But with Dax, she wanted something else. Everything. To see his muscles shift under sweat-beaded skin, to watch his cock slide slowly into her, to hear his pleasured groans as he came, to moan his name as she joined him.

Her voice was husky, barely recognizable when she half-asked, half-begged, "What were you saying about making it up to me?"

His eyes darkened with need as his gaze lingered between her legs, a fingertip barely touching her as it traced the seam of her sex. With a groan, he dove in, sliding his body against hers, trapping his cock between their bellies. Her insides clenched in anticipation of him finally entering her, or maybe in nervousness.

"Dax…" she muttered against a mouth that seemed intent on devouring her.

"I know. I should grab a condom before this goes much farther. There's a stash in the medicine cabinet," he murmured, clearly sensing her hesitation but not understanding why.

Even she didn't even really understand it. Maybe it was fear that they were moving too fast, the spiritual connection messing with them. Or maybe it was just her lack of experience. "That's not it," she muttered. "I've got birth control covered. And werewolves, like all supernaturals, are immune to human disease."

"Yeah? I guess that's something for the 'plus' column. But what if you're wrong and I'm not..." Dax trailed off, a frown tugging at his mouth when she bit her lip.

As his shoulders slumped, she realized she'd no desire to hurt him by pushing him to accept his fate. Now wasn't the time. "My last... Well, it was a while ago and he wasn't human. I'm clean," she admitted. "You?"

"Same here. Except as far as I know, you're my only nonhuman." He shifted his weight onto one elbow so he could trace his fingers along her jaw and down her neck before resting his hand over her heart like he wanted to feel its beat. "Witches are different, not human, right?"

Now didn't seem to be the best time to delve into what made her kind different. "For all intents and purposes, I'm like any other woman."

"I wouldn't be here with you now if you were."

Even as her mind spun with all the things he could mean by that, her heart swelled in her chest. She'd never ached like this for anyone. "Dax, I need you. Now." *Before I change my mind.*

"Patience, angel." He slowly slid down her body, his mouth and hands drifting over every inch, all the way down to the tips of her toes, before traveling upward again. He paused at the apex of her thighs, licking his lips.

Her whole body tensed in anticipation, her thighs quivering as conflicting instincts—to clamp closed or fall open—battled it out. Dax made the decisive move, slipping his shoulders under her knees.

His breath fluttered against the sensitive skin of her most private place. "I've been wanting to do this since waking up. Hell, since you raised me from the dead."

Was it possible for genitals to blush? Because she could feel heat flooding her nether regions.

Dax placed a soft kiss on the rise of her pelvic bone, gentle fingers opening her to him. When his tongue flicked out to taste her, then trailed over the entire length of her sex, Zelda's hips bucked. His low groan vibrated against her as his mouth closed over her clit. When her hips tipped wildly again, he slid a hand under her ass and pressed her tighter to him.

He bestowed the same level of attention he'd given her mouth to her most private bits, delving in with an expertise that curled her toes—long slow licks mixed with teasing ones, little nips, gentle suckling. It seemed that he'd hardly started when she felt a tightening deep inside, her whole body humming with the need for release.

Maybe it was the way her fingers tangled into his hair. Or how her trembling thighs squeezed his head. Or maybe he could read her mind. But he answered her unspoken need. One finger, then a second, slid inside her and curled upward, hitting a spot that left her moaning. *So close...*

It was the way he gazed up at her—the intensity in his lust-darkened eyes—that finally pushed her over the edge. Her back arched and her eyes slammed shut as she cried out his name, the release she'd been craving overcoming her. When she dropped back to the couch, she dared to glance down at him, sure he'd be bothered by how she'd crushed his ears against his head and ripped out some of his hair. But if his pleased, almost smug, smile was any indication, he didn't mind.

"God, you're beautiful." He placed soft kisses on the insides of each thigh before slipping out from under her seemingly boneless legs. He continued his soft, open-mouthed kisses over her pelvic bone, then trailed them up her body.

She could still taste herself on him when his mouth found hers. His tongue slid against hers, the head of his cock teasing at her entrance. Just a tiny shift of the hips and he'd be inside her. It was a dangerous game.

Dax freed a shuddering breath, tipping his head so their foreheads touched. His muscles were tense as if it was taking all his strength to stop himself from pushing into her. "You're still sure?"

Zelda answered him by cupping his face and pulling him down for a kiss. Wrapping a leg around his hips, she rolled him onto his back. They both froze, holding their breath as the head of his cock slid into her. The only thing keeping her from fully encompassing him was his grip on her hips. When she deepened the kiss, his hold loosened just enough for him to lightly trace circles against the soft flesh just inside the jutting bones with his thumbs. It sent a clear message—he wanted her but he'd follow her lead.

She tangled her fingers with his, dragging his hands above his head and pinning them to the couch. As she pressed down on him, her hips rolling slowly to draw him deeper, he sucked in a breath that pulled the air from her lungs.

"Oh God," Dax moaned, his teeth catching at her lower lip. His hips shifted against hers, his voice husky. "Zelda... I don't think I can take it slow. You feel too good."

"I swear, it's like you can read my mind."

Releasing his hands, she dragged her fingernails lightly along the insides of his arms, over his shoulders, and down his chest. He seemed to like it, a sound somewhere between a growl and a purr rumbling through him. His hips rose to meet hers as she picked up the pace.

Zelda let out a muffled shriek when his arm coiled around her waist, pinning her to him as he flipped her onto her back. His other arm hooked behind her knee, pressing it against his ribs as he continued to thrust into her.

Dax's mouth covered hers, a jumble of low curses escaping when she sucked his lower lip between her own and angled her hips so he could bury himself even deeper. After less than a dozen growly strokes, he pulled out and flipped her onto her stomach. Gripping her hips, he raised them and drove into her hard. Zelda cried out, equal parts pleasure and pain.

Dax paused, much to Zelda's frustration. "Fuck. You okay?"

"Don't stop," Zelda panted. "Please."

"Anything for you, angel." He nuzzled and nipped along her shoulders and the back of her neck, one hand massaging her breasts as the fingers of the other danced against her clit.

Her climax loomed, a tsunami threatening to sweep away everything in its path. She wanted to wait for Dax, but when he hit just the right spots inside and outside, his teeth clamping down on the crook of her neck, it rushed over her, sweeping her along in its wake. For one perfect moment, she felt something like she'd experienced at the lake when her and Dax's spirits entwined—felt him, completeness. She was only vaguely aware of his name escaping her in a long moan.

Dax's grip was the only thing holding her up. Each thrust was an exquisite form of torture, her body already building to another climax. His chest slid against her back, slick with sweat, his breath hot against her neck. He swelled within her, the strokes harder, faster as his end approached. Her whole body yearned for his release, knowing that it would push her over the edge again.

She wasn't sure who was trembling more, her or him. Dax's grip on her, both teeth and hands, walked the fine line between pleasure and pain. She imagined her own, more intimate, grip resided in that same realm for him. Maybe that was why he stopped moving, his breaths coming in ragged gasps and his entire body shuddering.

"Dax?"

But his only answer was a pained breath as he released her and scrambled away. Without his hold on her, she collapsed into a boneless heap, looking up just in time to see him disappear into the bathroom.

CHAPTER 7

FUCK, FUCK, FUCK...

Dax struggled for breath, staring down at his hands gripping the edge of the sink. He hardly recognized them —fingers gnarled and nails long and dark. No way in hell he wanted to look in the mirror, see what the reflection would show him. His teeth rattled in their sockets and his jaw ached like he'd played punching bag to a heavyweight, as did every other bit of his body. Some parts more than others.

He chanced a look downward. "Ache" was not a strong enough word—more like blue balls dialed up to eleven. He'd been on the verge of the best orgasm of his life when he'd been hit with the overwhelming urge to sink his fangs deep into Zelda's neck like a fucking vampire. The tip of his tongue slid cautiously along his teeth, stopping short at lengthened canines.

This can't be happening. I won't let this happen.

His body disagreed. Pain spasmed through him,

dropping him to his knees. Dax searched his memory for a time when he might have felt this bad. The annual Saturday training with his fight gym that always wrecked him for days afterward. The final time his last foster father had beaten him, breaking half his ribs. That time in juvie when he'd said no to the wrong guy, who'd then grabbed five of his buddies to jump Dax and put him in the hospital for nearly a week.

From the best I've ever felt to the worst in the space of a heartbeat—nothing comes close.

He groped along the counter until he found the edge of a towel. He pulled it down and crammed it into his mouth just in time to muffle the string of curses that escaped at the next jolt of pain. It shot down his spine and along his limbs, dropping him to his side on the tile. He rolled onto his back, letting warmth from the in-floor heating seep into him.

Oh God. Am I really a werewolf? Changing into a monster in Toby's house, with Zelda just on the other side of the door? She's not safe. What will I do to her? He'd seen enough horror movies to guess. How much longer until he tore through the flimsy hollow core door and mauled her? Even now, he wanted—no, *needed*—to bite her. And he very nearly had.

His tongue swept his lips, still tasting her there. The scent of sex and their mingled sweat clung to him. Desire flared again. And with it, the overwhelming need to plunge both his cock and fangs into her.

What the hell is wrong with me?

A dark chuckle rumbled in his chest. *I'm a fucking monster, that's what. And she's partly to blame.*

Isadora Kane's goons may have infected him, but it was Zelda who had brought him back, trapping him in a cursed body. Why had she done it? Maybe she wielded Karmic retribution like an archangel. Lord knew he'd been expecting that sword to drop for a decade. Failing to stop their foster father's abuse of Jennie and Jamie as soon as it started, then finally beating the man into a coma when he finally grew the balls to take a stand—a couple of years in juvie wasn't nearly enough punishment for that.

He still needed to balance the scales, do something good to counter the bad. But how could he do that if he was a monster? Maybe Zelda was the answer. She'd asked him to help save her sister, help them escape Isadora Kane. He'd known the moment she'd asked that he'd do whatever he could to help, his eagerness to leap into the fight catching him off guard. And forcing himself to sleep on it, to take some time before answering, had done nothing to change his mind. If anything, he was sure he'd do almost anything she asked, and not just because she felt like paradise.

That was a problem, almost as big as turning into a wolf. Zelda was convinced that she'd done something to bind them together, enslaved his soul, when she brought him back from death. As if to prove it, she'd tried to force him to slap her, her power a painful buzzing inside him, but he'd been able to resist, prove he was his own man. Werewolf. Whatever.

He couldn't deny the connection between them. But it felt as natural as breathing, not at all forced until she'd tried to use it against him. From the first moment Dax had looked up into Zelda's gentle eyes, he'd trusted her. Oddly, that hadn't changed once he'd realized his angel was actually a witch that talked to dead people.

His whole body clenched as pain chased through him again. He was a creature at war with himself. One part needing the comfort of her touch while the other wanted only to capture her, pin her to the tile floor, and finish what had been started on that couch. And that other part was winning control.

ZELDA LAY STUNNED and breathless on the couch. She'd heard of guys cutting and running after sex, but not right before they finished. Had she done something wrong? She was pretty sure Dax had been enjoying himself, up until he'd bolted.

But then everything about their encounter had been extraordinary. Zelda stretched, a shiver running over her as she ran a hand down the length of her still-humming body. *More like a transcendental experience than sex. Goddess help me, I think I left my body.*

Speaking of bodies... Now that she didn't have Dax to distract her and keep her warm—the man was the best kind of furnace—she noticed two things. First, it was cold enough in the basement that being alone and naked was uncomfortable. And second, he'd been rougher than she realized. She gingerly probed the stinging welts raised from his nails on her hips and the sore spot at the base of her neck where he'd gone beyond nibbling. From the bruised way it felt, Dax had given her one hell of a hickey.

Shit, if he broke the skin... The thought left her cold. She looked for any sign of blood on her hips while her fingertips explored the tender spot on her neck. *Clean.* She freed the breath she'd been holding. Becoming a werewolf-witch hybrid wouldn't further endear her to the coven. And then there was the Grand Coven and Council—they'd been looking for an excuse to sic the Enforcers on her.

The shiver that ran through her wasn't just from being cold. *Damn it, what's taking Dax so long?* Zelda wrapped a blanket around herself and slid off the couch. She padded across the basement to the bathroom, then knocked softly on the door.

"Dax, are you all right?" Pressing her ear to the wood, she waited for a response but heard only pained breathing. "Dax?"

She tried the handle. It turned, but before she could open the door more than a crack, he shoved it closed and locked it. She took a step back, glaring at the barrier as if that would make it open.

"You can't come in, Zelda." Dax sounded like he was forcing the words past clenched teeth.

"Convince me nothing's wrong, and I'll stop bothering you."

"You need to leave."

Zelda stared at the door. Did he mean back away from the door or something more, like leaving the house? "Is it something I did? What we—"

"No. Just go."

"Yeah, right," Zelda scoffed, trying to camouflage any hint of hurt. "I'm supposed to just leave without knowing you're all right? Let me help."

"You've already helped more than enough."

"What the hells does that mean? Please, just open the door, so I—"

"God fucking damn it!" Dax snapped. "I hate you so much right now."

Zelda cringed, ducking her head as if he'd slapped her. "I wish you'd told me that before you fucked me." She roughly rubbed away the welling tears as she slid down the door to the floor. "Why?"

Something scraped the other side of the door, opposite her head. It sounded like nails trailing against the wood. A soft thud followed the sound.

"You brought me back to this." Pain, or maybe something darker, deepened Dax's deep voice.

"This?"

"Life with this fucking curse."

"You hate," Zelda's voice cracked on the word, "me for bringing you back to life? Most people would be grateful for a second chance."

"Most people don't have a clue they could be brought back as monsters."

"You're not a monster." Zelda knew true monsters, and Dax wasn't one. If he was, he wouldn't be so upset about becoming a werewolf. She wrapped her arms around herself, pushing her next words past a tightening throat. "But you're right. I really messed up. I'm so sorry."

"Shit. No, I'm sorry." Dax paused and released a noisy sigh. "I don't know why I... I didn't mean it. Maybe it's the pain, like women cursing their partners in the delivery room. You should have heard the flaming my sister Jennie gave her husband."

"That's why you ran? Pain?" Zelda's fingers tightened on her upper arms. She'd never heard of First Turn happening so soon after being bit, but that would explain his disappearing act. Instinct could have driven him to hide, like an injured animal. "You're starting to shift?"

"Doing it doggie style is one thing, but I can't imagine you'd appreciate being humped by a wolf. Well, a werewolf." A groan interrupted Dax's dark chuckle. Even though he did his best to muffle the sound, Zelda still cringed in sympathy. He took a few noisy breaths before continuing. "Don't mind me. Just throwing a pity party now that I have a taste of what I'll have to deal with every month."

"Welcome to my world. Women have been doing it since the beginning of time."

"You're seriously comparing mood swings, cramps, and bleeding for a few days to transforming into a raging, blood-crazed monster every full moon?"

"For some, it's not a big difference. Don't knock the comparison until you've lived it."

"I could say the same to you."

"You don't have to be a monster. You can choose to be as docile as a golden retriever."

"Do I seem like the golden retriever type to you?"

No, more like a pit bull—all waggy-wiggle-butt and wide grin, until he decides to bite. Zelda rolled her eyes, knowing this debate wasn't getting them anywhere except annoyed. As much as she hated to upset him more, there were things he needed to know.

"Look..." she let her head fall back against the door, "I hate to be the bearer of more bad news, but the full moon was last week. The shift isn't limited to once per month. It can happen more often than that, triggered by extreme emotion or sensation. Kind of like what's happening to you now. I should have realized."

"Great," Dax half groaned, half grunted. "That makes me feel so much better."

"I'm sorry. If it helps, you can learn to control it. And while First Turn is a special kind of hell, it won't always be so terrible."

"Again, not helping. Can you do something to get me through it?" There was a note of desperation in Dax's voice. "Maybe you have something in your backpack that can knock me out."

"You need to be awake and aware when you go through the change so you don't lose yourself to the wolf."

"So, you're not going to help me."

"Of course I will." Zelda paused, trying to decide how much to tell him about what he was going to experience, what could happen. For the first time in her life, she actually wished Dimitri was there. He'd know what to say, to do. But then, he was also the one who created the problem. She took a deep breath. "Werewolves don't generally shift alone. They're with their pack during First Turn."

"You've seen it?" The relief was clear in Dax's voice.

"Yes. I was at the last couple First Turns. It's one of Isadora's conditions for keeping Larissa safe."

"Tell me."

Zelda bowed her head. Sitting like this, each of them on opposite sides of the door, able to hear but not see or touch each other, felt strangely freeing. She'd imagined it was how confessional would be. Anonymity, not seeing the judgment, or discomfort, on the other person's face.

"All werewolves go through First Turn. It's really rare, but for some, the pain is too much. Isadora thought it would be a good idea to have me there, to make sure no one dies, bring back anyone who does."

"So, I'm not your first." Was that disappointment she heard? Jealousy? Oddly, it didn't sound like fear. But then, he'd been dead once before.

"You were." Zelda swallowed hard. *My first, and probably my last...* "Like I said, it's rare. So far, everyone in the First Turns that I've attended has survived the process. Are you sure you want me babbling on about this?"

"Listening to your voice seems to be helping." Not that she'd know it from *his* voice, tight with pain. "Although, maybe you should move away from the door, or stuff something under it, so I can't smell you. Every time I get a whiff, all I want is to finish what we started. And given how bitey I got last time, that might not be a great thing."

Zelda lay her head on the floor and peeked through the crack. The dark eye peering back at her blinked in surprise.

"Zelda!"

"Sorry. Fine, I'll get something."

She climbed to her feet and padded into the storage

room, grabbing a few clean towels. She pressed them firmly against the bottom of the door before sitting down against it again.

"Better?" The only reply was a low grumbling that she couldn't quite make out. She took it as a yes. "As I was saying, First Turn is a big deal for werewolves. They think of it as rite of passage, a metamorphosis from a flawed form to a perfect one. Until Isadora decided to make a few changes, it was always a secret kept from those outside the pack. Although, most supernaturals understand it involves some sort of ritual and quality alone time with the pack's alpha. Traditionally, he acts as a tether, a focus during the pain of the shift, and provides instruction—a good deal for him since the initiate usually imprints on him that way." Or he ended the initiate's suffering quickly if the change went bad. "Afterward, the alpha presents the initiate to the pack and there's a 'beat in' of sorts, the new wolf fighting for his place in the hierarchy."

"Sounds awesome." Sarcasm was clear in his tone. "What did Isadora do that changed things?"

"She insists on First Turn happening at Coven House—she had a room specially built—and her being there. Dimitri is there too, but he's banned from interfering, mostly there to protect her. She wants to ensure new werewolves imprint on her rather than him. And she uses magic—*my* magic—to strengthen the tether."

"You've helped the witch bind werewolves to her, like what you did to me?"

"It isn't the same. I joined my spirit with yours, risked

my own soul. Hers... Well, it's a one-sided thing." It wasn't so much judgment in his tone but her own guilt that put her on the defensive. She wasn't sure if she was trying to convince Dax or herself. "I didn't have a choice. The things she was threatening my sister with... There are worse things than death. Or being bound to Isadora. And she doesn't have the power to force them to do anything they don't want to do. It's probably better for them. At least this way, they're in her good graces and likely to stay there."

"I understand having to do things you don't want to." Dax sighed loudly enough for her to hear through the door. "You didn't bring back a good person, Zelda. I was a monster long before you brought me back from the dead."

Zelda turned to kneel in front of the door, pressing her hands to the wood. "You're wrong. When our spirits entwined, I felt what kind of person you truly are. You're loyal, love your family, and do what's needed to protect them. Just like me with Larissa."

"It's not the same. You don't know what I've done." From the sounds on the other side of the door, she imagined him mirroring her stance. "Zelda, I'm scared. Even without claws and fangs, I can do a lot of damage. I don't want to lose control and hurt someone, hurt you."

"You can't go through your first shift alone. You need a tether, someone to help you keep a grip on your human side."

"Yeah, that's what I need—somebody watching me turn into a monster from a horror movie." Dax was silent for a moment, the only sound his pained breathing.

When he spoke again, his voice was gruff. "Could you do it? Be my tether?"

Zelda's heart swelled at the hope-filled question, but she did her best to ignore it. "I probably shouldn't. What if you imprint on me? It would only strengthen the link between us. And since you hate me—"

"I already told you I didn't mean it."

"And then there's your uncontrollable need to bite me."

"Definitely want to avoid that," Dax rumbled.

Zelda pressed her cheek against the smooth wood of the door. "But you'll need someone to stay close—keep you safe, make sure you don't have any problems shifting and have clothes to put on after. You don't want to be wandering around the woods naked this time of year."

"Probably not the best idea any time of year." Dax's voice on the other side of the door sounded like he was speaking low into her ear. "You believe me, right? That I didn't really mean what I said?"

"About?"

"About hating you. Out of all the people I know, you're the only one I'd want to have here while I go through this."

"You're just saying that because I'm the only one you know with knowledge of werewolves and the change, the only one not likely to freak out. And because you don't really want to go through it alone."

"That could be part of it. But it's not just that."

"Then what?"

"I don't know. I trust you, I guess."

"Well, thanks, I guess." Zelda took a deep breath. "If

I'm going to help you through this, you're going to have to let me in."

The silence seemed to drag on forever. "First you have to promise me you'll put clothes on, something more than those running shorts."

Zelda glanced toward Dax's flannel pajama pants and her T-shirt discarded in the middle of the floor. "Done. Although I recommend you stay naked." When there was silence on the other side of the door, except for the rasping of his breath, she reassured him, "No funny business, I promise. Trust me, you're not going to want anything restricting you, touching your skin. And if you're worried about me taking advantage of you in your naked state, I can assure you that it'll be easy to keep my libido in check once you start sprouting hair everywhere."

"Great. Just what I needed to hear. Thanks." He grew quiet again for a moment. When he finally spoke, there was no trace of humor in his voice. "There's something else, but I want you to agree before I tell you what it is."

"I can't do that."

"Just promise. Please."

Who was she trying to fool? She'd have agreed to just about anything to convince him to let her help. From what she understood, a werewolf's first shift into his wolf form took longer than any other, but if Dax's shift had started while they were having sex, he'd already fought it off longer than was advisable.

"I promise," Zelda vowed, forcing herself not to cross her fingers.

His dull, emotionless tone should have been a

warning. "Go into the storage room. In the northeast corner, on the top shelf, is a plastic case. The combination for the lock is seven, zero, three, six, eight. There's a Glock in there, already loaded, and extra clips. I want you to use it if I come after you."

"Or I could use the bear spray I saw in there instead." She didn't want to mention, let alone admit, her backup plan—she'd put his soul back into him, and she could rip it out. It was a last resort, one she hoped she'd never have to use. Just the thought of doing that to Dax left her feeling like she'd yanked out her own soul.

"It works on werewolves?"

"Sure, why not?" Or it could just piss him off more. But then, so would a bullet. Even an elephant gun wouldn't stop a werewolf.

"If you think it'll work." Dax sucked in a pained breath. "I think you better hurry."

Zelda rushed to yank on the pajama pants and T-shirt, then ducked into the storeroom to retrieve the bear spray. She stared toward the gun case, nearly hidden on the shelf. *Maybe I should grab it, just in case.* It would be one more way to slow Dax down before resorting to more drastic measures.

She set the bear spray canister down and climbed onto the bottom shelf so she could reach the gun case. Once she opened it and retrieved the gun, checking to make sure the safety was engaged, she shoved it and the canister into the pockets of the flannel pants. Their weight was enough to make the pants slip off her hips. She yanked them back up and retied the drawstring.

Returning to the bathroom, she knocked softly on the door. "You still you in there?"

"It's unlocked."

Zelda wasn't sure if she was happy to hear him answer with words. A part of her had hoped he'd shifted in her absence. She wasn't looking forward to watching him suffer, knowing she couldn't do anything to help him. She took a deep breath, steeling herself before cracking open the door.

Dax had wedged himself into the farthest corner of the bathroom. He'd wrapped a towel around his hips and sat with his knees tucked against his chest, his forehead resting on them. His shoulders rose and fell with rapid, pained breaths.

Dread was a cold ball in Zelda's belly as she cautiously approached. "I thought you'd be furrier."

He didn't look up when she knelt in front of him, but she heard something that might have been the start of a laugh. He let his knees fall to the side, crisscrossing well-muscled legs in front of him, then reached for her. "I promise I won't hurt you. They need to bite seems to have passed. Now I just need you close," he whispered.

She took his gnarled hand, going willingly when he drew her onto his lap and wrapped his arms around her. He tucked his face into the crook of her neck, the heat of his breath sending shivers through her, not fear but something just as deep.

"Is that bear spray in your pocket or are you happy to see me?" His voice was gruff, almost slurred.

"It seems *you're* happy to see *me*." The press of his hardening cock against her ass left her wanting to drop her pants and straddle him. "I thought we agreed to no sexy stuff. Although it might kick-start your change. Which we need to do. The longer you fight it, the more it'll hurt." And the more danger he'd be in.

"Hard to believe it could get worse." His head rose, golden eyes meeting hers.

Goddess help her, he was gorgeous, even on the cusp of his first shift. Exotic eyes stayed locked with hers as she traced her fingers over the bones of his face, his ears, and then his lips before raising them to get a better look at his fangs.

He reached for her hands, flinching when he caught sight of his own gnarled ones. Zelda couldn't even imagine how awful and terrifying it would be to see, not to mention feel, his body change. He almost looked relieved when her fingers closed around his and raised them to her lips.

"You'll get through this just fine." Thankfully, she sounded more confident than she felt. "The change has already started. You just need to relax and let it happen."

She felt his muscles spasm a heartbeat before he drew in a sharp breath. But instead of pulling away, she stroked his face and muttered soothing sounds. After several moments, she felt him relax.

"Easy for you to say," Dax rasped.

"No, not easy. I hate that you're in pain." Zelda kept her touch light as she continued to stroke him. "But it's as inevitable as birth and death. We just need to find a way to ease it."

"Having you here... It helps."

"I wish I could help more." She tried to climb out of

his lap, but he tightened his grip. "I'm not going far. I just want to make things more comfortable. You can't shift with me in your lap."

Once he released her, she set the bear spray canister and gun on the counter. She grabbed the towels and blanket from outside the door, using them to make a nest in the middle of the floor. Lowering herself onto it, she gestured for Dax to join her. The way he crawled toward her sent her heart thudding, the movement stiff and pained, yet oddly predatory. She forced an encouraging smile, patting the blanket next to her and somehow resisting the urge to say, "Here, boy."

Once he curled up on his side next to her, Zelda molded herself to his back, draping an arm over him. His heart pounded under her hand. They lay like that for what felt like hours as waves of pain washed over him, his body spasming and thrashing.

"God... Fucking shoot me," Dax groaned.

"It's almost over. You'll feel better once you change. I promise."

Dax flinched away when her hand rose to stroke his head, snapping, "Don't touch me." His tone stung, but she did her best to shake it off. When she moved back from him, he moaned, "Don't let go."

Zelda bit down on her lip, hoping to bottle the frustration wanting to burst out. "What do you want me to do?"

"The fuck if I know." Dax thrashed on the blanket, first curling into a ball, then cursing as he rolled onto his back. "I don't want you to see me like this, but I don't want you to leave. I want you to hold me, but it hurts too much."

Zelda focused her gaze on her fingers, twisting the hem of her T-shirt as she considered what to do. There was no good option. She bent down to kiss Dax's scruffy cheek, then turned to sit with her back to him. She reached behind her. "Give me your hand."

It took a moment, but his hand eventually bumped against hers. She wrapped her fingers around his wrist. "I won't look, but I'll stay here and won't let go. Work for you?"

Dax's response was little more than a growl, but since he didn't pull away, Zelda assumed it was a yes. When the time finally came, she held tight as promised. She kept her eyes clenched, her muttered prayers to the Goddess filling the room like a soft, thrumming heartbeat. The change took her by surprise, one minute her fingers against skin and the next fur.

When Zelda felt something large and furry bumping against her back, she opened her eyes and turned. Dax as a wolf was beautiful, golden eyes staring out from thick black fur. She released his forelimb and plunged her fingers into the dense ruff at his neck before moving up to trace the edge of a pointy ear.

His head cocked as if to say, 'Well?'

"You're gorgeous. How do you feel?"

He answered by swiping his tongue over her cheek.

"Don't get any funny ideas, fuzz butt." She winked, dragging a hand against her cheek as if to wipe away drool. Thankfully, there was very little. She pushed to her feet and turned toward the bathroom door, her body aching as if she'd also changed form. "You ready to try life on four legs for a bit? We could go for a walk." When she turned back to look at Dax, he was right behind her, a little unsteady but on all four feet. "And don't you dare sniff my ass."

His tongue lolled out between huge canines in a goofy-looking smile and his bushy black tail waved like a flag behind him. *Holy shit! I had sex with a guy who has a tail.* She almost tripped over her feet as his snout nudged her bottom. She yelped and shot him an annoyed frown. To be fair, the confirmation that she'd slept with a werewolf probably hadn't helped her coordination.

Zelda headed for the bar stool where she'd draped her jeans and wool sweater from the night before. She'd just slipped out of the flannel pants when a low growl rumbled behind her. She spun toward it, stepping back to put a bar stool between herself and the source. But Dax ignored her, his hackles rising as he glared at the window. He jumped onto the couch, stretching to paw futilely at the window crank.

"We'll go. Just give me a minute to dress and throw on my gear. I'm not built for frolicking in the snow without clothing."

But Dax's growling only grew louder, his clawing more determined, almost frantic. When she stepped toward him, he turned and made an angry sound that was a cross between a growl and a bark. She stepped back, holding her hands in front of her.

"Look, I don't speak wolf so I don't know what you're trying to tell me." She swallowed hard. What if the wolf inside him had taken control? "You're still Dax, right? Give me one bark for no, two for yes."

She didn't think it was possible for a wolf to roll its eyes, but Dax somehow managed something that was close enough before yipping twice. It was a clearly impatient sound, her interpretation bolstered by him turning his attention back to his assault on the window.

"If you break your friend's window, he'll never let you house-sit again. Not to mention it'll get awfully cold in here. Once I'm dressed, we'll head out."

His single bark was as emphatic a 'no' as she'd ever heard. "You don't want me to go out there?"

He yipped once.

"Is that no to me going outside? What's wrong? Is there something out there?"

Dax barked twice.

"Something dangerous?"

Two again.

"Goddess, give me patience! This is ridiculous."

She glared at Dax, planting her hands on her hips. His gaze drifting over her legs reminded her that she was naked from the waist down, while his expression clearly said, 'Tell me about it.'

"You shouldn't go either, then."

He didn't make a sound, just curled his lips to show enormous white fangs, then swung his head back to the window as if ordering her to open it.

"So, I'm supposed to just let you out, by yourself, so you can get hurt or killed by whatever is out there?" Zelda crossed her arms over her chest, her fingertips digging into her upper arms as if the pain could chase away her anxiety. "I don't want you to go."

Dax hopped off the couch, loping toward her. His nose was cold and wet against her leg as he rubbed his head along it. Her hand dropped to settle between his ears, mussing the fur between. The gesture seemed to give him an answer to a question she didn't even understand.

He circled her, rubbing one side of himself against her before turning and doing the same thing along his other side. Once he finished, he sank to his haunches in front of her. She wasn't sure what compelled her to do it, but she dropped to her knees and wrapped her arms around his neck, rubbing the side of her face against his before nuzzling into his ruff. He still smelled like Dax, just muskier.

Tears welled as she gave voice to her fear. "I don't want anything to happen to you."

He responded with a soft chuff before slipping free. As he moved back toward the window, Zelda hastily wiped tears from her cheeks. Her feet felt like lead as she shuffled across the carpet.

She climbed onto the couch next to Dax and cranked open the window, frigid air rushing over her. "Promise me you'll come back."

Dax gave her a quick lick on the cheek before disappearing out the window.

CHAPTER 8

IT TOOK A FEW MOMENTS FOR DAX TO ADJUST TO running on four feet instead of two. At least the snow and cold didn't bother him as much when he was wearing his very own fur coat. Although, snow between his paw pads took some getting used to.

It felt good to finally be running toward something instead of away. He just wished he'd been able to explain to her why he needed to leave. He'd find a way to make it up to her when he returned. The thought of her being there when he did lit a warm fire in his belly, like she was his candle in the window.

The sound of a wolf's howl, answered by a chorus just a heartbeat later, nearly stopped him in his tracks. The urge to raise his snout and join in nearly won out, but something inside warned him to stay quiet. They could be the same wolves that had killed him. Were they searching for him?

When he'd first heard them howling shortly after he'd

shifted, he'd feared they'd tracked him to the house, that Zelda was in danger. The last twenty-four hours had thrown everything he knew into doubt, but one thing was completely clear. He had to protect her.

The wolves' howling might be luring him to them, but he'd go on his own terms. The prickle of his hackles rising only added to the creeping dread as he neared his abandoned grave. The wind was in his favor, carrying the stink of wolves, freshly turned earth, and his own blood to him. The ones who'd killed him were there, the unique tang of their scent unmistakable. But he also caught the unrecognizable scents of others.

The pack. So, had they come to recruit or kill him? Neither appealed. He'd no desire to join them and become one of Isadora Kane's pets. Now Zelda's, on the other hand... He gave himself a moment to indulge fantasies of laying his head in her lap and her hands stroking him before refocusing on his immediate issue—the half dozen wolves in the clearing just ahead.

He crept in as silently as he could, wanting to see what he was walking into. Climbing onto the trunk of a downed tree near the edge of the clearing, he peered through an opening between the roots and dirt. Six pairs of eyes turned in the direction of his hiding spot. Somehow, they already knew he was there.

Fury stood his fur on end and drew back his lips as he recognized the wolves from the night before. They were bigger than he remembered. The one with darker, reddish fur seemed to be the leader—the alpha Dimitri—his head held high and his tail jutting skyward.

Instinct told him he shouldn't do it, but he met the

wolf's stare as he jumped off the downed tree and stalked into the clearing, holding his own head and tail high. The wolf to the leader's right—the title 'beta' popped into his head—shifted his gaze between the alpha and Dax, a low growl rumbling forth. But the alpha only looked Dax up and down, then gave what looked like the canine equivalent of a shrug. He released a low bark as he twitched his head toward the pair of wolves to Dax's left. The gesture reminded him of the one made by the guy in juvie, when he'd sicced his buddies on Dax.

It was all the warning he needed. He lunged out of the way just as a dusky-coated wolf surged toward him. Teeth snapped just shy of Dax's flank. He spun with a snarl, launching himself at the other wolf. His own teeth caught only the longer fur of the wolf's ruff.

They backed a step away, circling each other warily. Something in the movement reminded him of his opponent from the ring. Strange to think that fight had only happened the night before. If this was the same man, or werewolf, would he have the same weaknesses?

Dax charged in, his attack aimed for the other wolf's neck and head. And just like the fighter the night before, the creature reared his upper body back. While it didn't unbalance him as much as it would have if he was on two legs, it did leave his back legs unprotected. Dax's teeth closed around a limb, and he wrenched it to the side.

The other wolf yelped as he went down, his tail pressing against his belly for protection. Or maybe submission. Either way, Dax ignored it. He heard a satisfying snap as he shook his head. The other wolf's blood hit his tongue, and all he wanted was more.

Go for the throat, the deep, growly words sounded in his head like someone else spoke them. Or maybe it was just instinct given voice, driving him for the kill.

The other wolf's eyes widened as Dax lunged for his throat. The creature's forelimbs rose as if to ward Dax off, but he pushed past them. But before his jaws snapped shut on his prize, he felt something hit his shoulder. A tearing pain ripped through it as another wolf snatched him off his feet and flung him across the clearing. His back slammed into something immovable, hard enough that it knocked the air from him in a pained yelp.

As the clearing around him erupted into growls and barks, oddly reminding him of a canine version of fight night cheers, Dax shook his head and struggled to his feet. While it wasn't the first time he'd had to pick himself up after having the wind knocked out of him, it was more difficult now because he had twice as many feet to wrangle.

He was barely upright before the next wolf lunged at him. His snapping teeth and over-the-top snarling must have surprised the beast because he scrambled back out of range. As did the two others that had been closing in.

Dax kept the large cottonwood tree at his tail as he glared at the other wolves, daring them to come for him. They might have outnumbered him, but he wouldn't go down without a fight. And he wouldn't run, despite the memory of Zelda begging him to return tugging at him. He hated to disappoint her, but it didn't seem likely that he'd be keeping his promise.

The odds looked even worse when the beta shouldered the other wolves out of the way and loomed over him. The beast was twice his size. Even if Dax had spent time training to fight in his new wolf body, he still wouldn't have liked his chances of winning. He wasn't sure if it was stupidity or stubbornness that left him holding his ground, glaring at the beast.

Either way, the beta didn't seem to appreciate it. With something that almost sounded like a roar, the wolf ducked his head and charged. With that much telegraphing, Dax easily lunged out of the way, but the next half dozen attacks weren't so easy to avoid. But his smaller size had some advantages. He was quicker, more maneuverable. But how long before he misstepped? Once the beta had hold of him, he could kiss his fuzzy ass goodbye.

But he never had a chance to learn the answer to that question. He suddenly found himself snatched up by his scruff, his two-hundred-pound-plus opponent similarly dangling a couple feet away.

An enormous naked Russian, Dimitri, gave them both a shake. "Enough! He is one of us. No more fighting." He flung the other wolf away from him like he was nothing more than a dirty shirt. But he kept his grip on Dax, bringing him closer and taking a good sniff. "You reek of witch, pup. The necromancer, yes? The high priestess will not be happy. Wolves are not good enough for her precious daughters."

He sniffed at him again. "Too bad for you. She smells good. Almost as good as her sister." Dimitri's lip curled as he set Dax down and patted him between the ears. When Dax responded by snapping at his fingers, Dimitri cuffed him upside the head, nearly knocking him off his feet.

"You have spirit, pup. It is rare to survive First Turn without your alpha. But this we will discuss another time. You will take the necromancer a message. First, you are mine, not hers. Second, the high priestess demands a meeting. She will bring Larissa to the warehouse, tonight at nine. All will be settled between the high priestess and the sisters then."

He turned and strode away, seemingly unaffected by the cold, the other wolves falling in at his flank. Before he reached the edge of the clearing, he stopped and turned back. "Remember who you are, pup. Werewolf. Pack. We are a proud breed, not a witch's lapdog."

Could have fooled me, Dax thought. *I bet Isadora would disagree.* It was probably for the best that he couldn't speak in this form.

Dimitri shot Dax a glare, his lip curling in a warning snarl. "Careful, pup."

Shit, did he hear me?

Dropping forward, Dimitri completed the shift to wolf before his forelimbs connected with the ground. Snout in the air, he released a low howl, one the other wolves enthusiastically joined. Rather than give in to the urge, Dax turned and slipped into the woods.

He was anxious to get back to Zelda—they had things to discuss and plans to make—but he was also unwilling to lead the pack back to her. Hopefully, he'd be able to hold his wolf form as he drew them away from her.

ZELDA SAT cross-legged on the floor, staring into the

candle burning in front of her and fighting the urge to throw it across the room. Meditation had done nothing to calm her mind. Nor had cleaning, bathing, reading, checking in with Lucy, or playing games on her phone. Morning approached, and she was still alone.

Where in the hells was Dax? Her mind raced with all the terrible things that could have happened to him, alone out in the woods. What if he'd run into the pack? Or a wild animal? Or shifted back into his human form? He could be hurt or freezing. She bit hard on the inside of her cheek and shook her head to chase the thoughts away. Once she'd regained some semblance of calm, she plucked at the spiritual connection between them, urging him to return. Not that she was sure it even worked that way.

And where was Billie? Despite Zelda's summonings, the spirit remained noticeably absent. Zelda pushed back at the creeping edges of despair. She knew where it came from—loneliness, abandonment. She gave herself a few seconds to wallow, then steeled herself, determined to not give up. One more try to reach Billie, then she'd summon other spiritual assistance. She broke another section off her braid of herbs and used her ritual knife to prick her thumb, dripping three drops of blood onto the dried plants. She conjured the image of Billie in her mind as she lit the braid in the candle, infusing it with her will as she dropped it into one of her silver bowls. If the spirit was still in this realm, she wouldn't be able to resist.

She'd counted back from one hundred to sixty-six before she felt the vibration in the air. Billie looked strangely harried when she appeared, her finger-curled bob in disarray.

"Mistress?"

Zelda didn't bother to correct her. "I was worried about you, Billie. Where have you been?"

"Doing as you bid."

"And?" When Billie stared blankly at her, Zelda sighed. It wasn't like the spirit to be so difficult. Usually, she was happy to spill information. "Did you learn anything?"

"About?"

The exchange was starting to feel like trying to walk a cat on a leash. Zelda gritted her teeth. "About Larissa? Did you find anything at Isadora's office? Or by following the Russians?"

Billie's dismissive wave and tone were out of character for the spirit. "Larissa is not at Isadora's office."

"You were able to get past her wards?"

"Of course not."

"Then how do you—"

"I followed the Russian wolfs. And I saw your werewolf at his grave. He was with them, the pack." The spirit's energy was growing chaotic, her face pinching in anger. "And I saw you with him earlier. You have betrayed the coven, your kind, for a wolf. He will forsake you at the first opportunity, sooner if his alpha orders it."

Zelda could only gape at the woman. She understood the spirit's dislike of werewolves, but she was making a lot of assumptions about Dax. He was newly bitten, something he hadn't asked for, and had no connection to the old conflicts between witches and wolves.

"What did you see at the gravesite, Billie?"

The spirit rolled her eyes with a huff. So much for being the voice of reason. But before she could answer, there was scratching at the window. Zelda's heart stopped when she saw nothing but glowing golden eyes peering back at her through the dark glass. But fear quickly turned to relief.

"Thank the Goddess," she breathed. *Dax is back.*

She snuffed out the candle between her bloody thumb and pointer finger, then popped the stinging digits into her mouth as she moved the candle and silver bowl to the end table. Grabbing a folded blanket from the pile at the end of the couch, she shook it out to cover the upholstery before climbing up to open the window.

But before Zelda finished opening it enough for Dax to get through, Billie got in a last jab. "I will not help you betray the coven. If you side with the wolf, you are on your own." When Dax slipped through the window, the spirit shot him a glare—one Zelda was thankful he couldn't see—then vanished.

Zelda shut the window and the blinds before dropping back down to the couch. She tried to cover her sigh by wrapping her arms around Dax's neck and releasing it into his thick ruff. He smelled like cold air, spruce sap, and wet dog.

"I'm glad you're back. I was starting to worry." Zelda fought off a sneeze as his fur tickled her nose. "If you plan to stay like this for a while, we may need to give you a bath, though."

He gave her a canine version of side-eye as he turned in a circle on the couch and flopped down, dropping his head to her lap. His eyes drifted shut, his chest rising and falling with deep breaths as she smoothed a hand over his head and rubbed his cold ears, then raked her fingers through his dark coat. When they drifted to the denser fur at his shoulder, they snagged on something. He winced when she picked at it.

"What did you get into?" Whatever flaked off his black fur was rust-colored. "Blood?"

When he grumbled softly, she blurted, "Yours or someone else's?" Her fingers delved deeper until they reached his skin. It took her a few moments, but she found the already scabbed wound.

"Billie said you met with the pack. Did they do this?"

He barked twice.

"I hope you gave as good as you got." Anger lit her blood, fury building. Those damn wolves had no right to attack him. But then she remembered the final part of First Turn—the beat in. If that's what it was, he was now part of the pack. She shoved back at any unease. "It feels like it's healing fine. I'll look again once you shift back. You intend to do that soon, right?"

He gave her sad puppy eyes, his head drooping back to her lap.

"Hmm... I guess you wouldn't know how. To be honest, I'm not sure I know either. Have you tried thinking really hard about being back in your human form?"

She resisted the urge to shove him off the couch when he shot her the canine equivalent of rolled eyes. "It should happen on its own once you relax enough to fall asleep."

She slipped out from under Dax's head and squirmed into position between him and the back of the couch. Now that she knew he was safe, exhaustion set in. Grabbing the edge of the blanket, she pulled it over herself before draping an arm across his chest. "Want to give it a try?"

He stayed silent but didn't leave, so she took it as agreement. Her eyes drifted shut as her fingers slid through his fur. She could feel him relaxing with each stroke, his breaths slowing and deepening. It didn't take long before she joined him in sleep.

Dax woke to the heat of Zelda's body against his back and her hand absently stroking his belly. Judging by the slow, even breaths tickling his neck, she was asleep. As her hand drifted lower, his cock twitch to life, straining for contact. For a moment, he considered scooting up just enough to indulge the damned thing, but that would be all kinds of wrong while in his wolf—

His eyes flew open, his gaze raking down the furless skin of his chest. *I'm back to normal!* It took all his self-control not to jump up and down on his very human legs and feet in celebration.

Instead, he carefully rolled toward Zelda, wrapping an arm around her waist and snuggling in closer. A corner of her mouth curled upward, her hand slipping downward until it cupped his ass. She hummed contentedly as her fingers squeezed, massaged. After a few moments, they quested their way over his hip. When they wrapped around his hard-on, she made a little happy-sounding grunt.

Well, hell... my angel is frisky in her sleep.

Dax traced the delicate lines of her face, then the edges of her mouth, with a feather-soft touch, trying not to wake her. His fingers looked so dark against the ivory of her skin and pale blonde strands of hair. She was pretty in a Nordic princess kind of way—high cheekbones, arched brow, wide mouth, proud chin, upturned eyes. Women like her had always seemed cold and aloof to him. But not Zelda.

A plush, rosy lower lip jutted, begging for a kiss, as his fingertip swept over it. *As if I could say no to her...* He leaned in and brushed his lips against hers. Her lashes fluttered, startled blue eyes meeting his.

"Good afternoon," Dax said in a hoarse voice. *Thank God it didn't come out as a bark.*

"You're back in your human body again."

"Yup."

She swept her gaze downward, pink coloring her pale cheeks. "And naked."

"Umm-hmm."

"Mmm... nice. How do you feel?"

"You tell me." He looked down at her fingers still wrapped around his cock. "You planning to do something with that?"

"What?" She followed his gaze, the pink in her cheeks deepening. But she didn't let go of him.

"This would be better if you were naked too."

Her tongue swept the seam of her lips as she altered her grip on his length, her thumb sweeping along the ridge of its head, then over its tip. "You're not worried about a repeat of last night?"

It took him a minute to answer, his mind blanking as delicate fingers stroked him with the perfect amount of pressure. "Hoping for it. Without the wolf part. You?"

"Same." Her smile was enough to melt away any concern.

Dax threaded his fingers into her hair and molded his lips to hers. The gentle kiss quickly switched to something lustier, goaded by the insistent tangling of her tongue with his. Her grip on his cock tightened, the stroking of her hand matching the tone of her mouth, demanding.

He slid a hand down her T-shirt-covered side and flannel-covered hip. Too bad she wasn't wearing the shorts. Those he could easily push aside. He hooked the back of her knee, drawing it up to his waist. The heat at her center lured his trailing fingertips. When they delved through the fly of the pajama pants, they found only smooth warm skin. Continuing their journey, he slipped his fingers slipped into the damp heat between her legs. She groaned against his mouth, opening and angling her hips to give him better access.

So warm, wet. Perfect. "God... Zelda... I need to be inside you. Now."

When he slipped a finger, then a second, inside her and gently circled her clit with his thumb, she clenched around him. Her head dipped forward as she ground against his hand, her forehead resting against his collarbone and her breath hot on his chest.

When she stiffened against him—something he

suspected had nothing to do with the movement of his fingers inside her—he asked, "You okay?"

"You still smell like a wolf."

Dax turned his head toward his armpit and sniffed. He did smell a bit muskier than usual, but he thought it was better than post workout at the fight gym. Zelda's tone and the wrinkling of her nose left him thinking she might not agree. "Not surprising, since I am one. Does it bother you? I could hop in the shower."

"I don't... No... I—" Zelda blew out a frustrated breath, her frown deepening when she inhaled again. "It should." He almost cried when she let go of his cock and rolled onto her back. Her eyes turned toward the end table, avoiding his. "Billie said I was betraying the coven."

Dax felt something sink in his chest. Propping himself up on an elbow, he gazed down at her. Worry was clear on her face. "How so?"

Zelda bit at her lower lip, her fingers fidgeting with the hem of her T-shirt. "She thinks I'm siding with you, the werewolves."

"Since when am I on the wolves' side? Or on the wrong side of the coven? I know I pissed Isadora off, but—"

"You're a werewolf now, part of the pack." She jumped in before Dax could disagree. "Whether you wanted to be or not. Werewolves and witches are enemies—have been for longer than anyone can remember. I'm already inching along thin ice with the coven and Grand Coven because of the whole 'I-see-and-talk-to-dead-people' thing. Throw consorting with a werewolf on top of that..." She reached for him, her fingers hovering so close to his skin he could almost feel her touch. "I'd never do anything to hurt my coven sisters, but what if she's right? That I'm betraying them by...?"

"By what? Being here with me? Bringing me back to life and helping me through my first shift?" When Zelda stayed quiet, pressing her lips into a bloodless line, Dax sat up. His feet sank into the thick carpet, his toes curling into it as he fought the urge to storm away.

He bowed his head as he drew in a deep breath. "Funny... Supposedly, I'm an enemy of a coven I never even knew about until yesterday and you're betraying them for helping me. But it was your high priestess who started this by ordering *her* werewolves—from the pack that she's got pinned under her designer heels—to get rid of me. It's *her* that's holding your sister—a member of your coven—hostage to make you do what she asks. She's the one betraying your coven. You're cleaning up her messes. And if your coven doesn't get that, they're either stupid or just as leashed as the wolves. Maybe you're better off without them."

In the near silence that followed, all Dax heard was her breathing and too-fast pulse. When she sucked in a noisy breath and shifted on the couch behind him, he thought she was getting up to leave.

Instead, she leaned forward, pressing her hand to his shoulder and resting her forehead alongside it. Her breath tickled along his spine when she whispered, "I'm sorry. You're right. Isadora's the villain here. Not you."

"Or you." He took a deep breath. "Why didn't you tell me that she's your mother?"

"Stepmother." Zelda practically spat the word. "Who told you?"

"Dimitri." Dax couldn't help but chuckle at how closely his tone echoed hers. How many times had he, Jamie, or Jennie used that tone when correcting teachers or school counselors who mistakenly called their foster father, their 'dad'? "So, you're saying you have an evil stepmother. Like in a fairytale."

"Pathetic, right?"

"Who am I to judge? My parents left me in a basket on a doorstep. Well... to be honest, there was no basket, just a dirty old quilt, and they couldn't even be bothered to find a doorstep or church. Just left me like empty forty-ouncers on a picnic table in a park."

"Dax..." Her arms wrapped around him, her lips pressing against his shoulder. "I'm so sorry."

He was almost afraid to turn and look at her, not wanting to see pity. But when he did, he only saw sadness, like she knew how he felt. And seeing her looking that way broke something inside him. He cupped her cheek. "Me too."

Zelda pressed her cheek against his palm. "I know what it's like to not be wanted."

She really does know. Dax could feel it—that soul deep connection only found with someone who'd lived it. He drew her onto his lap, and she curled into him, her head nestling into the curve of his shoulder like it was meant to be there.

"And what it's like to be wanted." He dropped a kiss on the top of her head.

"We're quite the pair, you and me."

"Yeah, we are." He took a deep breath, drawing her tighter to him, wanting to feel her just a little longer. "I need to tell you..." He regretted that delivering the alpha's message would shatter their small bit of peace. "Dimitri told me to pass on the message that Isadora wants to meet at the warehouse tonight at nine. She's bringing your sister."

"Did he say anything else? Like what the meeting was about?" Zelda plucked her phone off the back of the couch and looked at the display. "At nine? Shit, it's almost four now. That doesn't give me much time to prepare."

"Dimitri didn't say much, other than the meeting would finally sort everything out between you, your sister, and Isadora." Dax took a deep breath. There was no need to tell her everything the alpha had said. The rest was between him and the wolf. "I've got a bad feeling about this meeting. I want to go with you, watch your back. Isadora will have her werewolf, and you should have one too, just to even the odds."

She leaned in to give him a light kiss. "Please don't take this the wrong way, but you versus Dimitri isn't even odds. I don't want you to get hurt."

"Too late for that." Dax felt the corner of his mouth curl upward. "Your ghost friend, Billie, said that you and I are on opposite sides. She's wrong. The only side I'm on is yours."

Dax didn't miss the glitter of tears in her eyes before they slipped shut and she bowed her head. When he nudged her chin upward to kiss her, she sank into him, her arms twining around his neck.

What was it about Zelda? He'd kissed a lot of women in his lifetime, but none of them affected him the way that she did. It was like she was Heaven and Hell embodied—bliss that left him aching, tempting him with more.

He groaned when she pulled away, but she shot him a soft smile. "What do you think of this—shower and finish what we started earlier, then eat as we try to come up with a plan for not dying at the warehouse tonight?"

Every bit of him howled yes, so he was just as surprised by his reply as Zelda. "That sounds great, but do we have time? I need more from you than a shower quickie."

Zelda's lower lip jutted, but she nodded. "You're right. Go take a shower, and I'll see what I can scrounge up to eat. If we take it to go, we'll have time before the warehouse for me to drop you off at home and head to Coven House to prepare for tonight."

"I'd like to see my family before"—he shook off the negative direction of his thoughts—"but I thought it was too dangerous for me to go home?" As much as he wanted to see them, his recent brush with death only making it seem more important, he couldn't help but question her change of heart. "I'm still going with you to the warehouse, right? This isn't just a way to ditch me?"

"Of course not. If all goes well, you and your family won't be in any danger from Isadora and the pack after tonight."

She took her sweet time sliding off him, as if daring him to grab hold of her. When she finally stood alongside the couch with an outstretched hand, the upward curl of her lips read like a challenge. As did the sensual swing of her hips as she led him toward the bathroom. She knew he was watching, and she enjoyed it.

Dax couldn't take his eyes off the hypnotic movement. His mind blanked except one thought: feeling that perfect ass grinding against him as he buried himself inside her. "I'm rethinking the shower quickie."

When she turned back toward him, her smile was equal parts shy and sensual. "Me too. But I don't want to keep you from your family." Gripping his shoulders, she stood on her tiptoes and leaned in to give him a lingering kiss. When she reluctantly pulled away, she nudged him toward the bathroom with a light smack on the ass. "Now get in there. You don't want to go home smelling like a stray mutt."

CHAPTER 9

Wɪᴛʜ ᴡᴀʀᴍ ᴡᴀᴛᴇʀ ᴄᴀʀᴇssɪɴɢ ʜɪs sᴋɪɴ, ʜɪs ʙᴀʟʟs aching with the need for release, and his thoughts lost to Zelda-centric fantasies, Dax gave in to the lure of a little self-love. Eyes closed, he stroked himself slowly, gently, imagining it was Zelda caressing him.

As if his wishing had conjured her, she was suddenly there, molding herself to his back as her arms slid around his waist. The unexpected press of her flesh against his nearly made him jump out of his skin—a reaction that could have been more literal than he'd ever dreamed.

Heat rose in his cheeks and his hand froze mid stroke, like a kid caught cramming a candy bar in his pocket at the corner store. For her to catch him, cock in hand... But her reaction wasn't what he would have expected—no shock or embarrassment, at least not on her end. Instead, he became suddenly aware of how thoroughly the scent of her arousal filled the small, steamy room.

"How long were you...?"

"Let me," she mouthed against his spine. Her fingers trembled as they interlaced with his, nudging his hand back into motion. "I didn't mean to interrupt. I just... Well, I couldn't just watch anymore."

God, she felt amazing, her skin slick and cool against his. His head bowed as he watched their joined hands stroke him. As good as it felt, he wanted more. With a groan, he uncoupled their hands from his shaft and turned toward her. Her sigh mingled with his when he drew her into his arms, her head tucking into the curve of his shoulder. The fingertips of one hand traced the geometric lines of the Aztec sun tattoo on his right pec, while the other hand smoothed up and down his spine, dipping just a little lower each time.

"Not that I want to chase you off, but I thought we didn't have time." All that silky skin under his hands, sliding against him, made it hard—pun intended—for him to concentrate on her answer.

"Once I got upstairs—saw there was nothing good to eat and realized how risky going to Coven House could be—I came up with a new plan. Assuming we get dressed and on our way quickly, don't run into any delays on the Glenn Highway, and get drive-through for dinner, we'd have approximately an hour for us and at least twice that for your family. Unless you'd rather spend more time with them, in which case we have time for a quickie at least."

"Umm-hmm. Good plan."

"Did you even hear what I said?"

"Got the basics. 'Sex now please,' right?"

"Close enough." She smiled against his chest. "You haven't gotten far with washing up."

"I was distracted."

"Understandable." She rose up on her toes and wrapped her arms around his neck. Small breasts and a taut belly pressed against him, trapping his cock between them. She nipped at his lower lip before drawing it into her mouth and sucking on it.

When he slid his hands down over her ass and between her legs, intending to lift her up, she pressed her hands to his chest and arched back from him. "Let's get you washed up first."

"But if we wash first, which *will* lead to sex, we'll need to shower some more, which will lead to more sex... A sexy kind of do-loop that I won't want to escape."

"You're right." A corner of her lips curled upward as she slipped free and took a step away. "I better leave you alone to wash."

Before she could take a second step, he tugged her back against them. Their naked skin connected with a wet slap. "I guess I'll just have to go back to what I was doing before you interrupted then."

Zelda peeled herself out of his grip with a groan. "Wash first."

She reached into the tiled cubby, pushing past the Irish Spring to grab a clear bottle of body wash. Dax recognized it as something Toby's girlfriend had given the guy for his birthday. While Dax had ribbed his friend about it, he knew it was out of jealousy. Not because of the girl or the gift itself, but because Toby had someone special promising him a night of sensual fun while Dax knew he'd be spending his night trying to decide if Jamie's latest fix up was worth the trouble.

Zelda is definitely worth the trouble.

She popped the lid on the bottle, a small grin tugging at her soft pink lips as she closed her eyes and sniffed. "Mmm... that's nice." She poured a small amount into her palm and rubbed it into his chest, seeming to enjoy playing peekaboo with his nipple and the lather, before rinsing it away. Again, she nuzzled into him. Her hum of approval vibrated through him as her mouth closed over his nipple, her tongue circling it before lightly biting. "Very nice."

Dax couldn't help but agree, assuming she wasn't talking about the scent of the body wash. What was it about vanilla, sandalwood, and amber—what the hell was amber, anyway—that women liked so much? Not that he was going to knock it, especially if it meant she was going to suds him up.

He stood still, mostly because she batted at his hands every time he reached for her, as she rubbed the soap into his hair and nearly every inch of him. Well, he'd certainly be the prettiest smelling werewolf in town. But watching Zelda get so turned on touching and exploring as she soaped him up made the perfumey smell, not to mention any potential teasing from the wolves and his family, worth it.

His voice was little more than a groan when he pointed out, "I think you missed a spot."

Zelda glanced down, pink blooming on her cheeks as she sucked on her lip. "I was saving that bit for last."

She slid from his loose grip to kneel between his feet.

Pouring some more body wash into her hands, she rubbed them together to work up a good lather. Her fingers worked the muscles of his calves and thighs, just as they had those of his upper body. An odd mixture of relaxation and anticipation shivered over him as her hands moved closer and closer to their goal.

It didn't take long before she finally reached it. Her thickly lathered hands slid over every bit of his cock and balls, even the area behind them. Her head tilted as she regarded his manly parts with an odd mixture of curiosity and something else—a part of him wanted to think it was awe. Even past the heavily scented soap, he could smell nervousness mixed in with her arousal.

For some reason, he couldn't stop thinking of videos he'd seen of snake charmers. He chuckled as he widened his stance a bit. "I promise it won't bite. You've got it completely under your power." When the blue eyes fixated on his cock widened, her tongue nervously sweeping across her lips, he continued, "It's okay, though. You don't have to..."

"To be honest, I've never really looked at a man's genitals, not like this. And I really want to do this but I've never... I don't..." She shook her head in obvious frustration, and drew in a deep breath. "You don't want me to?" Her gaze stayed fixed on his jutting cock—that part of him was clearly all for it—her small frown showing both surprise and disappointment.

"Oh God, I really, *really* do, but only if you want to." Dax brushed a strand of wet hair back and tucked it behind her ear before cupping her cheek. "I'd say explore all you want—Toby has a tankless water heater and claims that his well never runs dry—but we're on a tight schedule, right?"

She peered up at him, blue eyes blinking back mist from the shower. It was a little disturbing how innocent she looked in that moment. But with a quirk of the corner of her lips and her next words, the halo tilted. "I just want it to be good for you."

"I doubt I'll have any complaints." Despite his reassurance, she still looked nervous. Hell, he'd never had to talk a woman through a blowjob before. "Okay, a few pointers. Top one is no biting—a little bit of teeth is okay, but nothing too hard, especially near the head. Playing with my balls is great, but gently. And despite the name, it's more about sucking and licking..."

As he talked, blue eyes flitted between his face and his cock, curious fingers exploring him. She cupped his balls, rolling them gently in her hands before leaning in to press a soft kiss to one, then the other. Her eyes slipped shut as she drew one into her mouth. The wet heat as she gently sucked and rolled him on her tongue was enough to nearly undo him.

"Oh, God..." He sucked in a breath as he grabbed at the tiled cubby to keep his balance. He groaned as the heat of her mouth disappeared and she pulled away.

"Was that okay?"

It was a struggle to get the words out. "Better than okay."

"You don't want me to stop?"

"God, no. But I won't complain if you do that to my cock instead." When she regarded the jutting member, nibbling at her lip with her head tilted as if she was pondering, he continued, "If you wrap your hand around the base, use it like an extension of your mouth, it'll keep you from taking me too deep and gagging."

She wasted no time, her fingers wrapping around his cock, stroking him. "The skin is so silky, even more when it's wet," she whispered, her tongue sliding across the seam of her lips.

Her breath shivered over the ultrasensitive head as she leaned closer, her tongue flicking against the sweet spot on its underside. When he groaned approvingly—no way he could form words—she traced the rim with her tongue, then dragged it over the top to poke at the slit. He once again groaned his appreciation. But when she drew the head fully into her mouth, a string of curses slid free.

Her eyebrow arched, and he answered with a shaky smile. "Sorry. Feels awesome."

She blinked up at him, watching his reaction as she took more of him into her mouth. She must have liked what she saw because she took him in until he felt the tip of his cock bumping up against the back of her throat. It took a moment for her to coordinate the movement of her mouth and hand, and to figure out that varying her speed and amount of suction got the biggest response from him. Not that he didn't enjoy what she was doing in the meantime.

When Dax tangled his fingers in her wet hair and he could no longer keep from pumping his hips, Zelda grinned around him, fraying his control more. And when she surprised him by doing something with her tongue that pressed it against his sweet spot as she sucked hard, it brought him to the brink so fast that it almost hurt.

"Sweet fucking Christ," he groaned as he pulled free from Zelda's magical mouth with a pop, holding her at arm's length.

"I'm sorry."

"Oh God, no. Don't apologize," he panted. "That was great. I just... I almost came in your mouth."

She arched a blonde eyebrow. "Umm, isn't that the goal?"

"Usually, yeah." He dragged his hands over his hair as he stuck his head under the shower stream, fighting for control. "I didn't want to do that to you. I mean with it being the first time—"

"But what if I wanted you to?" She frowned, her eyes full of hurt. "Will you? Finish, that is. I really need you to."

"But what if...?"

"You're afraid that what happened before—you wolfing out when you're about to come—will happen again?" When he nodded, she rose to her feet, cupping his face in her hands. She peered into his eyes, lifted his lips to look at his teeth, and inspected his hands. "You look normal to me. And for the record, I've never heard of a bitten werewolf turning again less than twenty-four hours after their first shift."

"You're sure?"

"I wouldn't say it if it I wasn't. Dax"—she leaned in and kissed him, soul-achingly sweet—"I want to make you come."

"Like I could say no to you," he said, his voice husky.

When she started to kneel, he pulled her back up and held her close to him. He kissed her until they were both breathless, slowly walking her toward the wooden stool tucked into the corner of the shower. Taking a seat, he pulled her toward him until she was straddling his lap. He tightened his arms around her hips, nuzzling her breasts and suckling her nipples until she was squirming and panting.

She slid down until the backs of her thighs rubbed against the tops of his, their mouths melding as she ground against him. The silky heat of her skin teased against his length, each slide of her body a delicious kind of torture. Hell, they could probably both come just doing what they were doing. But his aching need could only be eased by burying himself balls deep inside her.

At the top of her next slide, Dax reached down and adjusted himself to line up with her opening. She slipped down him so slowly he could feel her stretching around him, so tight it bordered on painful. But she continued to take him until he was fully sheathed.

"Wait." Dax gripped her hips, holding her still. "You feel so fucking good, too good."

"Please. Let me." Her words could have been begging if not for her demanding tone.

He released his grip, glad to have his hands free to massage, stroke, caress. As she moved—head thrown back, skin flushed, pink-tipped breasts jutting toward him, begging for him to lick and nibble—he was sure he'd never see anything quite so beautiful again.

A part of him howled to take control, but he ignored it. Zelda seemed to know what he needed before he did— when to pick up the pace, take him deep and circle her hips, stop moving and focus on nothing but kisses. And as the pressure of his impending climax built deep within, she tightened around him, urging his release.

Never before had he felt so connected to another person, like he didn't know where he ended and she began. Hearts beat frantically, mouths devoured, hands grasped. And in that span of heartbeats when he exploded within her, the world seemed to stop around them.

The sound of her gasping breaths and touch of her hands was almost jarring, as if a reminder that they were separate beings. "Wow," she breathed against his mouth.

There was no need for him to say anything since she'd already said what he was thinking. So, he responded with a kiss.

CHAPTER 10

THE FIRST PART OF THEIR TRIP DOWN THE MOUNTAIN was quiet, both of them clearly deep in their own thoughts. Zelda wondered if Dax's thoughts veered in the same direction as hers—the cabin had become an odd sort of sanctuary, one she was reluctant to leave. But the chance to see, and hopefully rescue, her sister and the growling of her empty stomach left her foot heavier on the gas pedal than advisable.

Once they passed the water treatment plant, Dax asked to borrow Zelda's phone to call his family. She tried not to eavesdrop—that he conducted much of the conversation in Spanish helped—but Dax's tone only made her more nervous about accompanying him to his family's home. She didn't have to speak Spanish to understand they weren't happy with him.

"Your brother is pissed at you for disappearing?"

"Probably, not that he doesn't do the same

sometimes." Dax interlaced his fingers and stretched, his knuckles popping. "But my mom is furious."

Zelda glanced at him, not bothering to hide her surprise. "I thought you were abandoned as a baby?"

"I was."

"And?"

He took a deep breath, dragging his fingers through his hair. "Are you sure you want to hear this? It's not a happy story."

Zelda took advantage of the ice-free conditions of the highway to risk twining her fingers with his. "Yeah, I'm sure. You share yours and I'll share mine."

"Don't say I didn't warn you." The corners of his mouth tugged downward. Instead of pulling away, his grip on her hand tightened. "I spent the first fourteen years of my life bouncing from one foster home to another. I think it was home number four—I was about seven—where I met Jennie and Jamie. We were close in age and ended up bonding pretty fast. Once the social workers realized that we didn't act out when the three of us were together, they did their best to keep us that way."

Dax stared out the window, his voice carefully controlled and fingers twitching against hers. "Our last foster home was the worst one. The sick bastard got off on hurting us. It finally got to a point where I couldn't take anymore. The social worker and school didn't seem willing to do anything to stop him, so I did. While I was serving my time in juvie for assault, Jennie and Jamie's Aunt Carmen moved to Anchorage and took them in, adopted them. By the time I got out, she'd adopted me too."

"I'm sorry, Dax."

"Yeah, me too." His fingers squeezed hers, his voice so quiet that she almost didn't hear him. "What I said, about my foster father, doesn't bother you?"

When Zelda glanced over at Dax, he dropped his gaze to focus on their joined hands. Self preservation—she understood it well. He was worried that she'd reject him. "Do you regret it?"

"What? Beating the twisted fuck into a coma for what he did to us, probably did to other kids?" The sound of Dax's molars grinding filled the momentary silence. Zelda could feel his anger. It should have frightened her, but she could sense how tightly he kept it controlled. It was very different from the violent fury that drove Franklin. "No, I don't regret that as much as not stopping him sooner."

All Zelda wanted to do was pull the car over and hug him. "You asked if what you said bothered me. It doesn't. But what does is that you—a fourteen-year-old kid—were forced to defend yourself, your family, like that. That you lost so much of your childhood."

"It was rough, but I found my home in the end. I couldn't have asked for a better mom, brother and sister, not to mention my niece and nephew." That last part brought a full smile to his face. "I'd crawl through Hell for them. Everyone one should have someone to love, who loves them unconditionally." He turned toward her in his seat. "What about you?"

"I guess I'm still chasing my familial happily ever after." Zelda avoided his gaze, thankful for the excuse of driving. After what Dax told her, it felt silly to complain about her family. "You've met my evil stepmother, and I told you a bit about my grandmother and sister. My mom took off when we were little, driven away by my insistence that the dead are my friends. I haven't seen her since. And my dad, he's indifferent at best and an overbearing douchebag at worst. I haven't seen him in years, but he regularly telephones to remind me what a disappointment I am to him, to our lineage."

"And he doesn't care that your stepmother is holding your sister hostage?"

"He doesn't know—Isadora insisted on that. Not that it matters. He probably wouldn't do anything about it even if he knew. Coven politics."

"He'd put politics before family?"

"Most of the high houses do. Besides, he's making a new family in London now. As long as Isadora doesn't permanently damage us, he won't get involved." He'd turn the same blind eye toward Zelda if she didn't openly attack Isadora. She didn't want to imagine what he'd do if things went to shit at the warehouse. Zelda shook her head roughly, forcing a lighter tone. "So, tell me more about your niece and nephew."

They didn't stop talking until she pulled her Subaru into the driveway of a yellow duplex, parking behind an older, red Chevy pickup truck. They sat in silence for a moment, both staring at the building, tension making the air feel heavy, dense. She'd never met a boyfriend's family before, and this didn't seem like the ideal time to start.

"Maybe I should just drop you off, pick you up later."

"You trying to ditch me, angel?"

More like trying to avoid family drama. I've got enough of my own. "Look, you've clearly got things to work out with your family. That'll be easier without me in the way."

Dax raked his fingers through his hair, his eyes still glued to the duplex. "Yeah, I suppose that phone call sounded bad. But you staying might actually keep the yelling to a minimum. And if they start in, I'll get us both out of there. I promise, it'll be fine."

When she didn't say anything, his hand closed around hers. "They're good people, Zelda." He lifted it to his lips as he shot her a wink. "Besides, my mom is insisting that she meet the woman who could distract me so much that I'd forget to check in."

"You gave her only PG-rated reasons, right?"

He hesitated, his sheepish grin widening as she squirmed. He took pity on her at the same moment a statuesque, dark-skinned woman stepped from one side of the duplex onto the front porch. He shot Zelda another wink before pasting a chastised look on his handsome face. "Of course. I'm not an idiot. I can't help you at the warehouse if I'm stuck in a confessional at Saint Patrick's for the rest of the night."

He jumped out of the car, waving at the woman and shouting something in Spanish as he trotted toward Zelda's car door. He opened it and held out his hand, every bit the gentleman. His grip was tight as he escorted her to the porch, like he was worried she'd try to make a run for it.

"Mama Carmen, this is Zelda Melik, the one I told

you about on the phone. Zelda, this is my mom, Carmen Evans."

Dax's hand stayed glued to hers as Zelda reached out to take Carmen's offered one. The woman's dark eyes swept over her, more curious than critical.

"It's nice to meet you, Ms. Evans."

"Just call me Carmen. Please, come in." She gestured for them to move past her into the duplex. Dax opened the door, the spicy scent of jambalaya washing over them. He started to lead Zelda into the house when Carmen stopped him with a hand on his arm. "Dax, everyone's on your and Jamie's side. Why don't you gather them up? Zelda can help me get everything set up here for dinner."

Fear must have shown on Zelda's face because Dax's hand tightened around hers. "But—"

"She'll be fine, Dax. Just do what I ask."

When he nodded and bowed his head, Zelda fought the urge to flee. But Dax hit her with the sad puppy eyes, ensuring she couldn't. He leaned in and gave her a peck on the cheek, before whispering in her ear, "I promise, I'll make it up to you."

Those words reminded her of other times he'd made that promise, then made good on it. Zelda tried to ignore the insta-dampness between her legs. She whispered back, "Yes, you will."

Dax shot her a wolfish grin that told her he knew her secret—damned werewolf sense of smell—before bouncing over to the adjacent door, pulling it open, and shouting. "Uncle Dax is home! Where's my favorite rug rats!"

His announcement triggered high-pitched, earsplitting shrieks and what sounded like a stampede heading toward them. But Zelda didn't have a chance to see what was causing the ruckus because Carmen tugged her through the door and into the entry of her home.

The woman smiled as she shut the front door behind them and held out her hand for Zelda's coat. "I hope you don't mind me dragging you away from Dax. I thought you might need a moment before meeting the rest of the family. Dax has a way of working those children into a frenzy. Let them get it out of their system on the boys' side before you meet everyone."

She hung Zelda's coat on a hook next to the coat closet door and gestured toward the bench. Zelda toed out of her boots and set them under it, suddenly questioning keeping on her thick, knee high, yellow and black striped wool socks. It was probably ruder to go barefoot. Unfortunately, the socks clashed with her long bronze-colored skirt, which was still wrinkled and smelling of wax and various herbs from being at the bottom of her backpack. But Carmen didn't comment on her odd attire, just gestured for Zelda to follow her up the stairs into the main living area.

This side of the duplex was clean and cozy, the furniture plush and covered with pillows and blankets, not a hard edge in sight. Zelda could imagine curling up in a nest for two and watching a movie on the large screen television that dominated the wall between the kitchen and living room. Baskets filled with kids' toys lined the front wall under the picture windows, nearly overflowing with an assortment of stuffed animals, dolls, and colorful wooden and plastic blocks of various sizes and shapes.

Despite dinner preparation clearly being in progress, the kitchen was spotless, all white surfaces except for the colorful Spanish tile of the backsplash. Carmen gestured for Zelda to take a seat at the kitchen island as she headed for the giant pot occupying two of the stove's six burners. She picked up a large wooden ladle and stirred the contents for a moment before approaching Zelda to offer a taste.

Just as Zelda leaned in, Carmen asked, "What are your intentions with Dax?"

It was everything Zelda could do not to spray the contents of the spoon on the woman. "Intentions?" she sputtered.

Carmen gave her a look that was on the stern side of neutral as she quickly washed the spoon in the sink, then returned to stirring the jambalaya. "I have only known Dax for ten years, but in that time, he's become a son to me, no less family than Jennie and Jamie. How much has he told you?"

Zelda nibbled at her lip, dredging up the *CliffsNotes* version of Dax's life that he'd given her on the drive into Anchorage. She hadn't pushed him for more details than he'd offered, recognizing the wary stare of one recounting a difficult childhood. "Not a lot. Just that he was abandoned by parents and in foster care when he met Jennie and Jamie. He mentioned that their last foster parents were abusive, and that he hurt the man and had to spend a couple years in McLaughlin Youth Center in detention. And he told me that you're Jennie and Jamie's aunt and arranged for him to move in with you all after he was released, that you officially adopted all three of them."

"And that doesn't bother you?"

"What? His terrible childhood? Or him hurting the man that abused them and spending time in juvenile detention?" Something in the woman's expression suggested she meant both, or maybe neither. She wasn't easy to read. "I wish things had been different for Dax, for all of them, but I don't fault him for what he did. He was a desperate kid protecting the family he had. Given the hell he's been through, he could be an angry mess, but he's not. He's sweet, funny, gentle—"

"He was angry." Carmen frowned, her stirring picking up its pace. "Especially after they released him from detention. And it was more than recovering from being beaten nearly to death while he was in there. If anything, he seemed to think he deserved it. So much fury aimed at himself. Lord knows, I wish I could have gotten to those kids sooner. As soon as I found out what had happened, I came for them. They were all angry, didn't trust anyone but each other. And for good reason. It took a lot of time and prayer, but here we are."

All Zelda could do was nod in understanding. What little Dax had told her had made her childhood seem idyllic in comparison. And that was even if she included parental abandonment, an evil stepmother, psychopath spirits, a murderous abomination for a grandmother, vampires and werewolves, and the threat of execution by Enforcers constantly looming over her.

"I'm not trying to chase you off." Carmen's hand

closed on one of Zelda's shoulders, giving a gentle squeeze. "I just want you to understand what you might be getting into with Dax. He's a good man, but he has deep scars."

"I know." Zelda gave the woman what she hoped was a reassuring smile. She understood better than anyone possibly could, had felt his pain and anger when their spirits had intertwined. But she'd also felt his love and loyalty for these people, his family. Not that she could explain any of that to Carmen.

The woman gave her shoulder a pat. "I suspect you do." She returned to her simmering pot, gesturing with her free hand toward the cabinets to the left of the stove, then toward the adjoining dining area. "Would you please set the table? We'll need normal settings for six and the toddler dishware set up at the high chair."

Zelda nodded, following Carmen's directions as she offered vague answers to the woman's questions about her family. She'd just finished placing the last set of silverware when Dax rushed into the kitchen, his cheeks flushed. He wrapped an arm around her waist, whispering in her ear, "You okay? She didn't chase you off?"

"Not yet," she whispered back.

"Thank God. Brace yourself." He gave her a relieved smile followed by a quick kiss on the cheek. Keeping his arm around her waist, he turned her toward the footsteps and voices approaching the kitchen. "Zelda, this is Hope," he said, gesturing toward a grinning, rosy-cheeked, curly-haired girl who curtsied like she was meeting the queen. "My sister Jennie and nephew

Justice," he continued, indicating a woman who looked like a younger but less friendly clone of Carmen, hoisting a chubby-cheeked toddler on her hip. "And you remember Jamie," he said as he waved a hand toward his brother, who stared at her in surprise. "Everyone, this is Zelda, my," he bit his lip, ducking his head rather than meeting anyone's eyes, "friend."

"Girlfriend?" The young girl sidled up to Dax, giving Zelda a speculative look as she reached for his hand.

"Umm..." Dax and Zelda made the noise simultaneously. Heat rose in Zelda's cheeks. "It's very nice to meet you all."

"If we're going to eat before I have to leave for work, we better start," Carmen said, interrupting what was becoming an awkward silence. "Hope, honey, why don't you let Zelda sit next to your Uncle Dax tonight?"

"Only if she's his girlfriend," Hope chided.

Dax leaned down, scooping the girl into his arms. Whatever he whispered in her ear left her squealing. Hope grinned at Zelda with a gap-toothed smile over his shoulder as he deposited her in a chair.

She pushed dark curls back from her cheeks before folding her hands primly in her lap. "Uncle Dax can sit between us."

Dax was clearly fighting back a grin as pulled out a chair and gestured for Zelda to have a seat. Once he'd tucked her into the table, he sat in the chair between her and Hope. His hand found hers under the table, giving a squeeze before interlacing their fingers in a way that left his fingertips free to stroke her thigh. Luckily, it was a wooden table, hiding his affection from view. Although, the heat in Zelda's cheeks and angle of Dax's arm would probably hint to the adults at the table what Dax was doing.

As Jennie settled Justice into his high chair, she sent a critical look in Zelda's direction. "So, how did you meet my brother?"

Dax's touch was enough of a distraction that Zelda had to take a moment to remember what she should say. She was only supposed to coat-tail on the cover story that Dax and Jamie had dreamed up to avoid telling Carmen and Jennie that he'd been fighting.

"Umm... Jamie introduced us. We were all at the same party." Zelda had never been a convincing liar, and her nervousness at meeting Dax's family didn't help that.

"Oh? And where do you know Jamie from?" Jennie asked.

"Well, we'd just met at that party. He was chatting with the friend I'd gone with."

"Yeah, nice girl." Jamie smiled, although something about it made Zelda think he was up to something. "How is Lacy—"

"Lucy."

Jamie's grin didn't falter. "How is Lucy? I've been meaning to call her to set up that date we'd talked about, but I seem to have lost her number."

Was the man trying to blackmail them, using a night with Lucy as his ransom? What could he possibly think he knew that wouldn't also bust him if he spilled? Dax's fingers tightened, his thigh brushing hers as he aimed a kick in his brother's direction.

Zelda offered the man her sweetest smile. "I could

give you her number," she kept her expression steady as Jamie's smile widened, "but I wouldn't be doing you any favors. You seem like such a *nice* guy who deserves a *good* girl, and that's not Lucy. She eats guys like you for a post-midnight snack." It wasn't a lie.

Dax tried to stifle his laughter but was mostly unsuccessful. This time the kick under the table was aimed in his direction, catching her in its path.

"As if a 'good' girl would have anything to do with him," Jennie scoffed. "With either of you players." The look she gave Zelda was icy. "Great, so you met at some party a couple nights ago. But that doesn't explain where Dax has been since then."

"It's pretty obvious, sis," Jamie chimed in. "Someone's going to be spending a lot of time in the confessional."

Dax shot Jamie a threatening look before sucking in a deep breath. "Yeah, sorry about that. I got into it with a couple of drunk guys downtown after bar closing, lost my phone and coat and thrashed my clothes. Zelda played white knight, then nurse, saving my ass."

"You're hurt?" Carmen started to rise from her chair, her concern clear.

"I'm fine, mama," Dax waved her off. "Anyway, we went out for coffee and got to talking about our favorite places to explore. It turns out, she'd never been snowshoeing. When I told her that I knew of some great places up by Eklutna Lake and Toby had all the equipment we needed, she offered to drive. Since neither of us have to work until after Christmas, and I promised Toby I'd check in on his place while he's out of town, we decided to just stay up there for a bit—watching movies, snowshoeing, hanging out."

"Hanging out? Really? That's what you're calling it?" Jennie's scowl bounced between Dax and Zelda as she crossed her arms over her chest. "And here we were, worried about you while you were off 'hanging out.' You should have called."

"Like I said, I lost my cell phone and we couldn't use Zelda's—there's no cell phone coverage up there."

"You could have called us before you took off, or after on Toby's land line," Jennie countered.

Dax's fingers tightened on Zelda's as he leaned forward in his seat, frowning at his sister. "You know, Jennie, I *am* an adult. I'm sorry if I worried you all, but I'm allowed to 'hang out' with whoever I want, whenever and wherever I want."

Jennie opened her mouth as if to argue, but Carmen spoke before she could. "You're right, Dax. You're an adult and entitled to your privacy. But maybe the next time you decide to spend a couple days away from home, you'll at least let one of us know so we don't worry."

"But enough arguing. Let us pray." She bowed her head, gesturing for them to do the same. "Bless us, O Lord..."

Zelda watched them all through her lashes, saying her own silent prayer to the Goddess, wishing Dax and his family many more dinners together.

When Carmen finished, she opened her napkin and laid it across her lap before reaching for a steaming serving dish. "Let's dig in before the food gets cold. Hope, honey, why don't you tell us what you did today."

The girl sent a questioning look to each of the adults around the table. She took a deep breath as Dax dished jambalaya onto her plate, looking like she was charging up. When she opened her mouth, the words tumbled out so fast Zelda almost couldn't understand her. "Mima took us to the mall and we saw Santa. Well, not the real Santa. His beard was fake and coming off. And when I poked at his stupid pillow belly, told him it wasn't real, he said a bad word. And then Mima put Justice on his lap, and he screamed so loud..."

As Hope's story rambled on, Dax's fingers squeezed hers. When she looked up at him, he mouthed, "Thank you."

Zelda tangled her fingers tighter with his and offered a soft smile. It was unlikely he'd be thanking her later, assuming either of them had a later.

CHAPTER 11

Dax had been silent since they'd left his family's duplex. Zelda snuck a glance at him as she stopped at a traffic light. She couldn't read his expression, his profile stark against the dark window. When she saw the muscle twitch along his jaw, she reached out to close her fingers over his hand.

"Your family..." Zelda started, hurrying on when a frown tugged at Dax's lips. "It's obvious how much they love you, how much you love them. It's not too late. I can take you back home."

It was what she should do. As much as she wanted Dax by her side at the warehouse, seeing him with his family, how much they loved each other... She couldn't stand the thought of breaking their hearts if anything bad happened. Funny how this man had gone from a weapon to something more, someone she cared about, in just a couple days.

"I wish Carmen had been our first mother. Between

Jennie, Jamie, and me, we went through almost a dozen foster families before she took us in. But she's done her best to make up for lost time, to help us heal some nasty wounds. And she's been an incredible Mima to Jennie's rug rats, giving them the kind of childhood we didn't get."

"They're adorable." Zelda's heart thrummed with the memory of sweet Justice nuzzling into the crook of Dax's neck and rowdy Hope swinging from his arm when he took them downstairs for bedtime. It was enough to make her ovaries ache. "You're really good with them. I'm sure they wish you'd stayed to read them a story."

"Green light." Dax's fingers twined with hers, his other hand gesturing for her to drive. "I'm not their dad, but I do what I can. Tucking them in will have to be enough this time."

Zelda turned her eyes back to the road. "You're a good uncle, and Jamie seems to be as well. But Jennie must be counting the days until her husband returns."

"This is Dave's third tour in the Middle East. You'd think they'd be pros at the separation by now. But I've seen the calendar Jennie keeps in her nightstand, heard her crying alone in her bedroom after one of their calls. Not that she'd ever admit it." Dax's fingers tightened on hers. "It's funny. I used to get annoyed with her. She knew what she was getting into when she started dating a military man. Despite knowing he might be shipped off, or even killed, she married and had kids with him. But I think I can understand now why she'd be willing to put herself through such hell."

Zelda tore her eyes from traffic to look over at Dax. He flashed her a smile before raising her hand to kiss the back of it. *Damn it!* Why couldn't he have stayed the hot but indifferent jerk she'd originally thought he was?

"I can't let you do this," Zelda blurted.

"What?"

"Put yourself in the middle of this."

"This?"

"The insanity that is my life."

"It's not that crazy. Sure, there's your evil witch stepmother, hostage sister, home filled with witches and werewolves, and friends who are ghosts. But that just makes for exciting holidays. I'm invited to Christmas dinner, right? Because I'd do anything to be there."

"I'm serious." Zelda sighed. "This is life-and-death levels of dangerous. Isadora orders her wolves to kill people. You need to escape while you can."

"I think I understand the life-and-death part of this better than anyone." The smirk was clear in Dax's tone, but it softened with his next words. "And it's too late. I'm already deep in it."

"But you don't have to be."

"I've got claws, fangs, and a tail that say otherwise. This isn't all about your feud with your stepmother, or the way I feel about you."

Zelda's mouth went dry, her words barely more than a whisper. "Which is?"

"Worth exploring, assuming we survive tonight's adventure. Do you agree?"

Her heart thudded. It wasn't like she expected declarations of love since they'd only known each other for a couple days. If he'd said the words, she'd have thought it was their spiritual link talking. "I'd like that."

"Great!" His smile made its way into his voice. "Then I'd like to take you out tomorrow night on an actual date. How about dinner and a movie? Moose's Tooth pizza and *Star Wars*?"

"And if I said I didn't like either of those things?"

"God, I hope you're kidding." When Zelda only smiled in response, he laughed. "If you were serious, I'd be heartbroken but I'd deal. I guess we have a lot to learn about each other. I don't even know where you work, or your favorite color, or if you cry when that Sarah McLachlan ASPCA commercial comes on."

When Dax lit into an off-tune rendition of the song from the commercial, lingering on the word 'angel,' Zelda felt tears rise, and it wasn't just from his bad singing. "Stop that! Is there anyone who doesn't?"

"I bet Isadora and Dimitri don't."

"Funny you should say that. Dimitri volunteers at the Alaska SPCA. One of my coven sisters caught him there when she was visiting in search of a familiar."

Dax snorted, "Probably to find his next snack."

"You might be right." It was difficult to imagine that the alpha had a heart. Zelda turned down the deserted industrial street that led to Mabon Enterprises' warehouse. "Too bad time's up. We'll have to save the twenty questions for our date. I'm sure it'll make for riveting dinner conversation."

Time's up. The words hung in the silence of her Subaru as she pulled up next to Isadora's BMW, parked in front of the warehouse. This was the night. Either Zelda, Larissa, and Dax walked free, or she'd have to resort to drastic measures. The question was, how drastic would she dare to go to ensure their freedom?

When she parked the car and unbuckled her seat belt, Dax reached for her, his fingers closing around the nape of her neck to tug her closer. Pressing his forehead against hers, he whispered, "No matter what happens tonight, I want you to know that I'm grateful for you giving me back my life and the last couple of days."

"Me too."

Dax's lips brushed hers, light as the breath he freed. "Ready to rescue the damsel?"

"Shit!" Zelda cursed under her breath—although not quietly enough for Dax's newly enhanced hearing to miss —as they walked through the steel double-door entry to the warehouse.

"What?" Dax tucked her behind him as he pulled her to the side of the entry and scanned the dim space. From Zelda's tone, he half expected to see the pack, crouched for attack. When he saw nothing but empty metal folding chairs, he let the door shut behind them. And with it went any light except the soft red glow of the exit sign above them.

His ability to see in the dark had improved since turning, but he couldn't see into the shadowed, near pitch black areas outside the dim light of the sign. The only sound was Zelda's rapid heartbeat and shallow breaths, echoing his own.

He breathed in through his nose, the sharp tang of

Zelda's fear under the lingering sweet smell of body wash making him draw her closer. His nose told him there were others in the warehouse. Dimitri's musky scent nearly overpowered the softer ones of two women, one who smelled like the Nordstrom's makeup counter and the other whose delicate earthy and herbal smell reminded him of Zelda. There were traces of the rest of the pack underlying it, but the scent had dulled enough that he guessed they were no longer in the building.

"The warehouse is warded." Zelda's whisper was thick with tension. "I won't be able to call upon any spirits for help if things head south."

"So, scratch Plan A. Got it."

They barely made it a half dozen steps from the door before the floodlights over the cage flipped on. Once his eyes adjusted, he saw what had made Zelda suck in a breath. At the ring's center, a woman slumped in a metal folding chair like the ones surrounding the cage. Despite the blonde waves curtaining her face and shoulders, Dax was sure she was the bound woman from Isadora's office. If there had been any question that the woman was Zelda's sister Larissa, her reaction answered it.

Dax caught her arm when she lunged toward the cage, halting her and tugging her back to his side. She tried to pull free but he held on. "We shouldn't go rushing in. That's what they want, putting her on display like that. Let Isadora and Dimitri show their hand first."

For a moment, it seemed she was going to resist, her eyes narrowing and a frown furrowing her brow. Despite the tight muscle of her lean arm, it struck him how delicate she seemed. Like if he squeezed too hard, she might break. He loosened his grip, sliding his hand down until he closed it around hers.

"Well, isn't that sweet." Isadora emerged from the hallway leading to the locker room area with Dimitri at her flank.

She didn't look like she belonged in this rough place. Sauntering in with her designer outfit and sky-high heels, she looked more like a polished business woman, better suited for a skyscraper boardroom in Chicago or New York. Her hand smoothed over her sleek updo as she said in a sickly-sweet voice. "You were right, Dimitri. Grizelda has ensnared a new boyfriend. And a handsome wolf at that."

"Grizelda?" Dax murmured out of the side of his mouth.

"It's an old family name," Zelda grumbled. "I'm sure Dax is short for something equally heinous."

"Nope." A corner of his mouth curled as he looked at her. From what he understood, his name had come from initials carved on the picnic table where he'd been discovered. All things considered, it could have been worse.

When he leaned in close to her ear, trying not to chuckle as he whispered "Grizelda..." in his sexiest tone, she rewarded him with an elbow to the ribs and pink rising in her cheeks. "Not sure I'm feeling it, angel."

"Focus," she hissed.

Oddly, her order had the opposite effect—unless she meant for him to be thinking about moaning that name during sex, and her leaving him with things unfinished because of it. If she was having similar thoughts, she kept them to herself, shifting her focus between her sister and stepmother.

"What did you do to Larissa?"

The woman walked the red runner to the ring like she was on a fashion runway. Her pencil skirt hardly seemed to have enough give as she climbed the metal stairs leading into the cage, the clicking of her heels echoing through the warehouse.

Dimitri remained her hulking shadow. Everything about him, from his expression to the way he moved, screamed that he was one wrong move away from exploding into violence. Something inside Dax cowered, but he locked it away. There was no way he was going to roll over and show his belly to that bastard, alpha or no.

Isadora stepped up behind Larissa and stroked her hair, although the gesture didn't look particularly tender. "What do you think of the latest spell I've added to my grimoire? It's my very own take on a Sleeping Beauty curse, but with a twist. She can only be woken by a werewolf."

When Dimitri stepped toward Larissa, Isadora brought him to heel with her sharp tone. "Not you, idiot. Our newest pack member will do it."

Dimitri's lips curled into a toothy snarl as all eyes turned to Dax. "He is nothing. A weak pup."

"Thanks, big guy. Good to know you're a fan. I mean, I did kick your boy, Hunter's, ass on two and four legs." Dax glued a smirk to his face when the alpha's glare turned in his direction, keeping eye contact as he asked, "Why me?"

"Because I wish it." Isadora turned her cold green

stare toward Zelda. "If you want your sister back, you will convince your pet to do this. Since you are linked, he must do as you say. That is the way it works, if I recall."

Zelda sucked in a breath. "How do you—"

"How is dear Franklin, by the way?" The woman's burgundy lips curled upward.

"Franklin?" Dax turned toward Zelda.

"I'll explain later." She glared at Isadora. Dax had never seen Zelda look so murderous, but then he hadn't known her long. For all he knew, it could be a normal expression. Or maybe it was one reserved for her stepmother. Hopefully, he'd never see that scowl pointed in his direction. "He's not important."

"It would devastate him to hear you say that, Grizelda. You know his only purpose is fulfilling your wishes. He loves you with all his heart, or he would if he had one." Isadora turned her gaze toward Dax. "My daughter is a fickle girl. You would do well to keep that in mind."

"The only thing Franklin loves is chaos and destruction," Zelda shot back. "And don't call me that."

"You cut me to the quick, child. Larissa has never objected to me calling her daughter. Such a sweet, loving girl."

"And look what that got her." Zelda's fist was clenched so tightly that Dax could smell the blood from her fingernails cutting into her palms. "And to think, we actually liked you in the beginning. Hells, we wanted to love you, for you to love us, be a mother to us."

"As if anyone could love you, child. Your dark power, your ties to death, will forever make that impossible."

Dax gave Zelda's hand a squeeze as he took a step forward. "That's bullshit."

"Aww... is the wolf smitten?" Isadora sneered, dark glee lighting her eyes. "Well, guess what, Romeo. The only reason you feel anything but disgust for her is because you're bound to her. Even her own parents couldn't wait to get away from her."

When Zelda's hand went limp in his, her shoulders slumping, Dax squared his. "Don't listen to her. This bitch doesn't know what she's talking about."

Zelda sighed. "No doubt you're right about my mother, but it was your scheming that chased my father off. Well, that and the lure of the much warmer bed of a pretty priestess on the other side of the pond. Say that three times fast." That last part she added under her breath. "You may be high priestess of Sleeping Lady Coven, but you didn't earn that title. You've never cared about any of us outside of how we can serve you."

"And I suppose you can do better?" Isadora moved nearer to Larissa, closing her hands on the younger woman's shoulders. "I know what you've been doing, Grizelda. Talking to the others, trying to turn them against me. But imagine how horrified sweet Larissa and your coven sisters will be when they learn that you raised the dead and bound this wolf to you."

"You're insane!" Zelda slipped from Dax's grip, striding toward the cage. "We have more important things to talk about—our lives, loves, dreams—than you. But you've never bothered to learn anything about us except how best to use us as weapons."

"They're terrified of you. They know you'll snap just like your grandmother and try to destroy them all."

As Zelda made her way around the cage toward its opening, Dax could smell the power building in the space, like ozone. It drifted over him, leaving his skin itching and the hairs on the back of his neck rising. A glance toward Dimitri told him the alpha was feeling it too, his fists and jaw clenching.

"You're the one trying to destroy us," Zelda snapped. "How many people's lives have ended on your orders? How long until the authorities find a body and tie it to the pack, then to you? You risk exposing us all." She turned her glare on the alpha. "You're a brute, Dimitri, but I don't believe that you're an idiot. You can't want that for your pack. You'll be hunted, exterminated."

Before the wolf could answer, Isadora stopped him with a raised hand. "You can't turn him against me. You bound him to me."

Dax gaped at Zelda. He knew about her part in binding the newer wolves, but the alpha? The wolf who killed him? He was starting to realize there was a lot about this woman that he didn't know.

Her face paled as she avoided his gaze. "I didn't take away his free will, just made it so he couldn't harm you. And I was an idiot to do it."

"You did it because you know everything I do is for the coven, that I will make us invincible."

"No, everything you do is for you, to further your own power. You're like some kind of witchy mafia boss with your wolf henchmen." Zelda gestured toward her sister, then the bristling alpha. The air around her hand

183

shimmered with power. "You use us, witch and wolf, with no regard for consequences."

"Enough! I demand your loyalty, obedience." Isadora placed her hands on either side of Larissa's head, and the young woman's hair shifted around her shoulders as if a wind was moving through the cage. "I can make this coven great, more powerful than any other."

Dax stepped onto the stairs leading into the cage, pushing past Zelda. "And I thought I had family bullshit to work through." He raised his hands in the air when Dimitri stepped toward him, ignoring the glares of the two conscious women in the building. "You said this spell could be broken by a werewolf, that you wanted me to do it. So, tell me what I need to do, Ms. Kane. I'm ready to be done with this crap and get on with my life, such as it is."

Isadora arched an eyebrow in his direction before turning her gaze back to Zelda, who had moved to stand at his side. "I'm tired of fighting with you, child. It's a distraction I can't have if I'm to proceed with my plans. Let's set aside this old bitterness and discuss why I brought you here—our future."

"I just want my sister back. Let her go and we'll leave. The coven will be yours."

"I can't allow that. The coven, certain magic that surrounds it, requires Melik blood, your family line, to sustain it." Isadora took a step back from Larissa, gesturing to Dax that he should approach. Frown lines furrowed her brow when he didn't move, deferring to Zelda for his next move. "I have a deal for you, Grizelda."

Zelda sighed, the noise full of frustration. "I can't wait to hear it. Your deals have been so great up 'til now."

"I'll ignore your lip, child. This time." Isadora brushed a loose strand of hair back from her forehead. "Swear to me that you'll stay and help me achieve my goals, and I'll let your sister and this pup leave."

"What's the catch?"

"They must leave Anchorage and not return."

"I'm not leaving." Dax crossed his arms. As much as he wanted to help Zelda and her sister, this was asking too much. "I have... too many reasons to stay.

"You're just not going to be happy until everyone is as miserable as you, are you?" Zelda shot back at Isadora.

Dax's fingers closed around Zelda's arm and he tugged her toward the edge of the cage. "There has to be something else we can do," Dax whispered softly enough that only Zelda could hear, putting as much hope as he could into his tone. "What if I agree to this, but we all make a run for it after Larissa wakes up? I have a friend who has a place just outside Homer. We can hide there for a couple weeks until everything dies down. Then I can come back, convince my family to leave."

Zelda shook her head, taking a shuddering breath. "You know they won't leave, and you can't stay. The pack will catch you. There's another option."

Her hands closed around his forearms as if steadying herself. She leaned in close, her cheek brushing his. "I don't care what you have to do, but once Larissa is awake, get her out of here. Don't look back. If I'm able, I'll meet up with you at Toby's. But if I don't show up by morning, get her out of town, someplace safe. Tell her to contact the Council, tell them everything."

"Zelda, what—"

"Promise me, Dax. You owe me a life. I'm calling in that debt." When he nodded, she brushed her lips against his cheek. She stepped past Dax and faced her stepmother. "Fine, Isadora. You get what you want. As soon as Larissa is awake, I'm all yours. But you have to promise that Larissa, Dax, his family, and the coven will all forever be safe."

"You and your pet do as I say, and I will." Isadora's smug grin left Dax questioning her trustworthiness.

Dax's jaw dropped. "Wait! No, that's not what I—"

"Do as I say, wolf," Zelda demanded, gesturing like she was tugging on an imaginary leash.

There was power behind her words, but nothing like what she'd hit him with before. When she shot him a subtle wink, he tried not to let sudden realization show on his face. She wasn't surrendering or trying to bend him to her will. She must have a plan in mind, needed him to play along. He bowed his head in what he hoped looked like submission, fighting the urge to mutter, "yes, mistress."

A cold ball of dread grew in Dax's belly as he stepped away from Zelda and walked toward Larissa. Crouching in front of her, his face level with hers, he brushed her hair back. She looked like her sister, just younger and more generically pretty. But it was Zelda's face he wanted to cup in his hands, her lips he wanted against his.

"So eager to kiss the girl, pup?" Isadora gloated.

"Like I said before, I just want to get the hell out of here. If that's what it takes..."

Dax shot Zelda an apologetic look, not that she took it that way if the crease between her eyebrows and tight line of her lips was any indication. *Well, the sooner I get this over with...* He pressed his lips to Larissa's. He hadn't expected fireworks, but he'd expected something to show he'd broken the spell. There was nothing.

"I thought you said I could wake her?"

"I didn't say a kiss would wake her. This isn't some fairy tale, and you're no Prince Phillip." Isadora's light chuckle turned dark. "No, pup. This spell requires something a bit more involved. Just a little nip." She raised Larissa's arm and pulled back the sleeve, presenting her wrist to Dax. "And it doesn't have to be someplace scandalous. It just needs to be deep enough to draw blood."

"No! If he bites her—"

"Shut up, Grizelda. A deal is a deal. Another word from you and I'll have Dimitri rip your pet's pretty head from his neck." She presented Larissa's wrist to Dax again. "Do it."

She waved a crimson-nailed hand in Zelda's direction when Dax didn't move. "I only need one of them. Do it or I'll have Dimitri bite Zelda. And I'm sure he won't be gentle. He holds no affection for her."

As Dax took Larissa's arm and bent toward it, all he heard was an annoying buzz in his head. Was Zelda trying to stop him through their connection? The memory of his and Zelda's first time together popped uninvited into his head, the pinching in his gums as the urge to bite her had risen with his climax. But he felt no such urge this time. He gave his head a rough shake before closing his mouth over Larissa's wrist. Bile climbed his throat as still human teeth scraped against skin that smelled slightly of chamomile and some other herb he didn't know.

Just a little bite and this will all be over, right?

DON'T DO IT. *Don't do it. Don't do it,* Zelda chanted in her head, forcing her will through the connection between her and Dax. If he bit Larissa, he'd infect her with the werewolf curse. After what he'd been through, how could he not realize that? Be willing to inflict that on another? But as if moving in slow motion, his head dipped closer and closer to Larissa's arm. And when his mouth latched onto her wrist, she had to press a hand over her mouth to keep from screaming.

But before Dax could bite down, Dimitri rammed into him, sending the smaller man flying into the chain-link surrounding the cage. He stalked toward Dax, who was struggling to get back up, delivering a kick that doubled him up and audibly knocked the air from his lungs. Turning his back on the downed man, Dimitri returned to Larissa. He lifted her from the chair, carrying her to the opposite edge of the cage and gently laying her down.

"I am alpha." Dimitri shot a glare at Isadora. "I decide who is bitten into the pack and how. I decide who my wolves take as their mates."

Dimitri held Larissa's hand like he was going to lay it on her chest. Instead, he pressed the back of it to his cheek in an oddly tender gesture. Could he have feelings for her? Zelda didn't have time to think about the answer before he struck at her sister's arm like a cobra.

Zelda screamed, rushing toward Larissa. But Dax got there first, launching himself onto the alpha's back.

"We weren't finished," Dax grunted as he coiled an arm around the larger man's neck.

As Dimitri pawed at Dax, trying to dislodge him, Zelda knelt at her sister's side, examining the bite on her arm. It was little more than a nip, hardly bleeding. She pulled the scarf from around her neck and wrapped it around Larissa's wrist, pressing hard to stop the trickle of blood. Less than a minute passed before the woman's eyes fluttered open.

"Thank the Goddess! Are you all right?" Zelda pulled her sister into a tight hug. "Of course you're not. I'm so sorry. I didn't want this for you. I'm sure we can find—"

Larissa wiggled out of Zelda's grip. "Dima?"

Dima? Did Larissa mean Dimitri? Zelda held her sister at arm's length, shaking her to get her attention, but the woman only had eyes for the men fighting on the other side of the cage. Zelda couldn't blame her.

So far, Dax seemed to be holding his own, deftly avoiding the larger man's punches and grabs. But for how long? And if Dimitri managed to catch him... Zelda shuddered at the thought.

Now that Dimitri's bite had broken Isadora's spell, it was time to enact her Plan X—a plan of last resort she hadn't shared with Dax. Zelda extended her spirit, reaching out to the others in the room. They glowed with life, so different from the ghosts she was accustomed to. Taking a deep breath, she coiled her spirit around Dimitri and Isadora's, pinning them in place.

"Dax, get Larissa out of here," Zelda cried out.

Dax stared at his suddenly unmoving opponent, fury clear in the tightness of his body and growling breaths. His lip curled into a snarl as he took the opportunity to kick Dimitri's knee, dropping onto his chest as soon as he hit the mat. Fingertips sprouted claws as they wrapped around the alpha's throat.

"Stop!" Zelda gasped. "You need to get Larissa to safety. I can't hold them for long."

Truthfully, she'd no intention of *holding* either of them. Every fiber of her being cried out for vengeance— for Larissa and Dax, the countless others hurt by the high priestess and her werewolves. She envisioned ripping Isadora and Dimitri's spirits from their bodies, casting them into oblivion. The thought made her gut churn and bile rise in her throat, but she swallowed hard, tightening her spiritual grip.

Isadora had been right about one thing—Zelda terrified her coven sisters, not to mention most who met her. They saw the truth. She now sensed that Isadora and Dimitri knew it too. She was Death.

But the last thing she wanted was for Dax to see her as anything but his angel. "Get. Larissa. Out. Of. Here. Now." Zelda infused the words with as much power as she could spare.

Dax's head snapped up and he wiped a bloodied

hand across his eyes. His mouth opened in surprise, or maybe warning, just as Zelda heard a woman scream behind her. Her hands flew to her ears as she spun toward the piercing sound.

She stood frozen, her grip on Dimitri and Isadora's spirits faltering as she faced Larissa and the high priestess. At first, she wasn't sure what she was seeing. It was something out of a bad horror movie—a bloodied fist protruding from Isadora's otherwise pristine pink silk blouse. Her perfectly painted lips formed an O, her scream now silent. The hand disappeared with a sickening squelching sound, and the woman collapsed bonelessly to the mat.

Larissa stared down at her arm, covered with gore to her elbow, and then stepped gingerly back from the spreading crimson puddle at her feet. The ridiculous thought popped into Zelda's head: *Who the hell is going to clean up this mess?* A sound like something between laughter and sobbing accompanied the thought, and she realized it was coming from her.

She should go to her sister, but before she could move, a dark blur blazed past her. Dimitri was going after Larissa! It made sense that he'd want vengeance against the creature who killed Isadora. The hells if she'd let that happen.

But before Zelda could react, Dax's arms banded around her waist, so tight she could hardly breathe. She thrashed, kicking and screaming, needing to get to Larissa, to protect her, but Dax held her tight. Deep, soothing sounds vibrated against her back, his hand stroking her hair.

Dimitri's arms closed around Larissa, but instead of tearing her to shreds, he pulled her against his massive chest. The woman stood, stiff as a corpse, until the huge Russian muttered a single word. "Risa."

She collapsed against him, her hand leaving a trail of gore across the back of his shirt. "Oh, Dima. I did it. She won't hurt anyone ever again. Not me, not you, not anyone. We're free."

The young woman's ranting blended with the Russian wolf's rumbling until it was an incoherent buzz in Zelda's ears. She reached for a tether, finding it in Dax's soothing tenor and steady heartbeat. Strong arms held her tight, heated breath and lips ruffling the hair on top of her head.

"It's done. Over. We're safe," Dax repeated, the words battering against any doubt.

Zelda turned and wrapped her arms around his chest, squeezing hard enough that his words turned into a pained groan. "Sure. Safe. But seriously, who's going to clean up this mess?" she croaked. Not just the actual mess, but the rest of it. The coven's high priestess had just had her heart ripped out by a witch-turned-wolf, bitten by the local alpha who seemed to be in love with her. That would not go over well with the Grand Coven or the Council.

"Larissa. She's... I need to—"

"She seems to be safe now. And apparently right where she wants to be." A dark chuckle rumbled through Dax. "Don't worry, angel. We'll figure it all out. In time."

CHAPTER 12

As Zelda and Larissa argued and Dimitri found a quiet spot to call whoever one called to clean up high priestess remains, Dax ripped down the red curtain that separated the main public area of the warehouse from the restricted areas in back. He draped it over Isadora Kane's body, fighting the urge to cross himself and say a prayer. He doubted the witch would appreciate such a thing.

"Zelda, please," Larissa begged, "Let me go with Dimitri."

"I don't understand why I can't come with." Zelda gripped her sister's shoulders, giving the woman a little shake. "It's not like I've never been through a First Turn before. I got Dax through his just yesterday."

"This is different—"

"No, it's not. I need to be there, make sure nothing goes wrong, that you don't—" Zelda's voice cracked and she shook her head roughly, rubbing at her eyes. "I just got you back, no thanks to that fucking wolf, and now he wants to take you away again."

"Don't talk about Dima that way. It's because of him that I'm still alive. He took care of me, protected me, woke me from Isadora's curse. And *he* doesn't want to take me away, *I* want him to. I need him to." Desperation added a sharp edge to Larissa's quiet voice.

"Why?

"I just told you. Goddess, why don't you ever listen to me?"

While Dimitri tried to stay out of the discussion, Dax couldn't any longer. He moved to Zelda's side, wrapping an arm around her waist. She stiffened for a heartbeat but didn't pull away. Dax took that as a good sign.

Maybe that was why he pushed his luck, guiding her a few steps from her sister and leaning in, speaking softly so only she could hear. "Zelda, your sister has been through Hell. God knows what happened to her while Isadora held her captive. And in just the last hour, Dimitri bit and infected her with the werewolf curse and she shoved her hand through Isadora's chest. *And* she's starting to turn. That's a lot to deal with. Let her and Dimitri deal with it."

"And that's exactly why I need to stay with her. This is Dimitri's fault! If he hadn't bitten her—"

"She'd still be under Isadora's curse." Dax peered over Zelda's shoulder, then turned her to face her sister. The woman had curled into Dimitri's tree-trunk-sized arms, completely peaceful for the first time since he'd woken her from Isadora's spell. Dax leaned in to whisper in Zelda's ear. "Look at her, at them. She's been stumbling along the line of sanity since Dimitri woke her, only coming back to her senses when the alpha is at her side, is touching her. He *is* helping her." What he didn't bother mentioning was Dimitri's obvious concern about Larissa, something they were all feeling.

Larissa looked up to find Zelda and Dax watching her. "All I want is to go to the cell at Coven House and complete First Turn with Dimitri. *Just* Dima. Why can't you let me do that?"

"Why can't you just let me help you?" Zelda tried to move toward Larissa, but Dax held tight.

Larissa freed a frustrated sound that was part growl, part roar. "Goddess, you're beyond dense! We need to be alone so we can finish our mating. The last thing we need is an audience, especially a judgy one!"

Silence descended for a moment. Zelda's entire body trembled, a volcano building to eruption. "No! I can't let that happen."

Larissa's eyes widened like Zelda had slapped her. She finally managed to sputter, "You don't have a say in this, Zelda! Fate has chosen this for me."

Dimitri drew Larissa deeper into his embrace, the witch looking fragile in his grip. He was surprisingly gentle, but his face showed considerable strain. Even Dax, a new werewolf, sensed how desperate the situation had become. The delay from their arguing meant that Larissa would not make it to Coven House, that her First Turn was going to happen at the warehouse. And they didn't have much time.

He heard a deep voice rumble in his head, *Get her out of here, pup.*

Great, now I've got the bastard in my head. When the alpha curled his lip, flashing an impressive amount of fang, Dax nodded to the werewolf and tossed Zelda over his shoulder, heading for the exit. He paused at the double doors, not so much because Zelda was fighting him, but because he didn't want the sisters to part from each other angry. He gave Zelda's rounded rump a bite. Her yelp echoed through the warehouse, but she stilled.

"Tell your sister you love her and will see her soon," Dax fought the urge to bite her again, just for himself this time. The scent in the building was having an effect, making it almost impossible to think about anything other than getting Zelda naked and plunging himself inside her.

Zelda sucked in a noisy breath, her hip bones grinding into his shoulder as she arched up to look at her sister. "I'm sorry, Larissa. I really do just want what's best for you, for you to be happy and safe. I'd pay any price to ensure it."

"Dimitri makes me happy. He's what I want. I love him, Zelda. And I love you." Joy was clear in Larissa's voice.

Dax could feel Zelda's body relax, even if her voice sounded strained. "I love you, Larissa, no matter what. You're sure?"

"Surer than I've ever been about anything in my life. Now get out of here before you see something you can't unsee."

"Promise you'll call as soon as you can?"

"Of course. Seriously, get out of here," Larissa promised.

Zelda flopped back down, giving Dax's ass a tap. "Get me out of here."

Dax hurried out the door and to Zelda's car. He set her down next to the driver's side of her Subaru. She didn't say a word, her jaw clenching as she dug her keys out of her bag and unlocked the doors.

Dax climbed into the passenger seat, watching Zelda buckle her seatbelt and start the car. He buckled himself in. "She'll be fine. Like you said when I was going through it, things rarely go bad during First Turn. And traditionally, the alpha was the only one there. Dimitri will make sure she gets through it."

Zelda's eyes narrowed as she stared at him. "That wolf killed you, tore you to shreds and left you in a shallow grave. But I'm supposed to trust him with my sister? Would you trust him with yours?"

"To be honest, I don't know. But if he looked at Jennie the way he looks at Larissa, I'd try."

Zelda didn't answer, and she stayed silent the entire drive to his house. When she pulled in behind his pickup truck, he released his seatbelt and turned to her, covering her hand, which was white-knuckling the steering wheel, with his own.

"Come inside." Dax tried to keep any sort of desperation out of his voice, a surprisingly difficult thing to do. All he wanted was to keep her close. "We can have a drink or two, talk. Or watch a movie if you don't feel up to talking."

She stared out the window, but her eyes were dull, like she wasn't looking at anything. "I should head back to Coven House, tell my sisters what happened. We need to arrange funeral rites and decide who will be the next high priestess. And someone needs to report what happened to the Grand Coven, to the Council, to my father." On that last bit, Zelda's voice trembled.

"You sure?" When she nodded, he continued, "Maybe I should come with. You shouldn't be alone—"

"No, it's better if I am right now."

"You're mad at me."

"No." She turned to him, pulling her hand free and slipping it behind his neck to pull him to her. Her cold nose was a sharp contrast to her warm breath on his neck. "This wasn't your fault. It's mine."

"It's Isadora's." Dax wrapped his arms around her, pulling her tighter to him. For a moment, the world felt right again, the events at the warehouse drifting away like the remnants of a nightmare. "Zelda, I—"

She silenced him with a needy kiss, leaving little doubt of her intent. And as much as he wanted her, he wasn't entirely convinced that screwing her in the front seat of her car while parked in his family's driveway was a good idea. Although, all she wore under her skirt was her panties and heavy wool socks that came up past her knees, so they wouldn't even have to undress. Just a quickie to help them forget for just a few minutes.

No, she deserved better. It took all his self control to pull away from her, but he was unwilling to go far. He rested his forehead against hers. "Come inside."

He grew dizzy, holding his breath in anticipation of her answer. When she shook her head and retreated back to the driver's side of the car, it escaped him in a mournful sigh.

"I need to go." Her voice was hoarse, like she was fighting back tears. "I'll call you tomorrow, okay?"

He nodded, his tightening throat keeping him from saying anything. It was probably for the best.

DAX PULLED his pickup into an empty parking spot on the street in front of the office building where Mabon Enterprises was located. Had it really been less than two weeks since he'd last been there? It felt like an entire lifetime had passed since then. In a way it had—he'd died and his new life had begun. Unfortunately, an important part of that new life had been missing for the last week.

He sat in his rapidly cooling truck and stared up toward the third-floor office. He knew Zelda was there. Her Subaru was parked in the lot on the back side of the building. There was no way he was going to ignore the opportunity to see her again, to ask her why she'd been ghosting him for the last week.

So much of what had happened since the last time he saw Zelda was a blur. The events at the warehouse had taken a toll on everyone. They probably needed a few days to process it, to deal with their new realities. But Zelda was the only one still avoiding him. She hadn't returned his calls or texts. Even Larissa, who'd been chatty with him all week, had been tight-lipped about her sister, only sharing the same things she told the rest of the pack—that Zelda was the new high priestess and boss at Mabon Enterprises, and that things might change between the coven and pack.

When he'd finally showed up at Coven House, worry nearly driving him out of his mind, her friend Lucy had happily invited him in. Not that she'd been any more helpful than Larissa. She clearly had other things on her mind, practically coiling around him like a boa constrictor. He'd had to threaten to wolf out on her before she'd backed off and admitted that Zelda wasn't there and wasn't due back for hours. She'd pointed him toward Mabon Enterprises before slithering off to harass one of the other werewolves.

At least Lucy had done him one favor—proving to him that his out-of-control libido had nothing to do with his inner wolf. The pretty witch's aggressive attentions did nothing for him, while just thinking about Zelda made him crazy.

Enough was enough. Dax jumped out his truck and strode through the main door, up three flights of steps, and then to the end of the hallway. His hand closed around the doorknob of Mabon Enterprises' office. He took a deep breath, one that filled him with her scent— God, the things just a whiff of her did to him—as he opened the door. Zelda was there, leaning against the edge of the desk with her back to the door. Her slender body was silhouetted against the dimming afternoon light on the other side of the window. She didn't turn when Dax cleared his throat.

He rubbed his clammy palms against his jeans, glad she wouldn't be able to smell his nervousness. The scent of it was only feeding into his own anxiety. "I hope I'm not interrupting anything. Did you get my message? Well, messages. I'm not used to playing stalker."

Zelda pushed away from the desk and walked toward the window, leaning against the frame. "One of the things I like about this time of year, besides the amazing sunrises and sunsets, is the ravens. I've been watching them for the last hour, swooping and playing. Have you ever seen such a thing?"

Dax moved to stand behind her, following her gaze. A dozen of the large black birds soared around the top of the twenty-plus-story Hilton Hotel—diving at each other, tumbling through the air, and then soaring upward to do it all again. "I've seen it, but I can't remember the last time I stopped to watch. Mostly, I just get annoyed at them for tearing into anything I stick in the bed of my pickup."

"They were harassing magpies on the roof of the Federal Building earlier. Their antics entertained me so thoroughly, I completely lost track of what the Board of Directors was saying. Luckily, it was a teleconference, and I could blame my lack of focus on ghostly visitors. It's not like that's far from the truth. I've actually considered putting Isadora's wards back up."

Zelda peered over her shoulder, her gaze sliding over him before focusing on a point near the door. A crease formed between her blonde brows, the corners of her mouth tugging downward. "I told you, Billie, it's my decision. Would you please give us a moment of privacy, and keep any other spirits from interrupting?"

She sighed and turned back to the window. "I hear you've been busy. Congratulations on winning the position of pack beta."

Dax's heart thudded once, then seemed to stop. He'd

been nervous about telling her, knowing she'd worried about how the coven would react to her being with a werewolf, that they'd see her as a traitor. And now that he had rank within the pack, there was no denying his loyalty.

He didn't know what was going on in Zelda's head, or her heart, but he knew he couldn't stop thinking about her. When Dimitri had strong-armed him into a fight for beta, his first thought had been to wonder what she'd think. While his body was still adjusting to the curse and aching from the recent fight, he still craved Zelda's touch, as if he knew on some instinctual level that she could make everything better. And when Dimitri and Larissa had spent hours cramming his brain full of information about werewolves and witches and other things that went bump in the night, not to mention the dynamics between them, he'd wished it was Zelda instructing him. Yeah, he had it bad.

Unfortunately, the powers that be had long ago forbidden witches and werewolves from mixing. What Isadora had done, bringing the coven and pack together under one roof and cause, was unheard of elsewhere. Would Zelda go back to the traditional ways? Was that why she'd been avoiding him?

Dax stepped in closer. He needed to be near her, to touch her. He took it as a good sign when she didn't flinch from his hand brushing the small of her back. "More like beta understudy, I guess. Yuri is still beta, but who knows when he'll be back from wherever he took off to. How did you—"

"Larissa and Dimitri told me before they left town for

their honeymoon, or whatever newly mated werewolves call it." She turned toward Dax, her hand rising to his face, her fingers brushing the nearly healed injuries that still marked his face. "They said it was quite the fight, that you almost—" Her voice broke on that last word, and she ducked her head. "I'm glad you're all right. I'm sorry I wasn't—"

"I'm glad you weren't." When Dax heard Zelda suck in a pained breath, her hand dropping to her side, he rushed to explain. "It was brutal. And from what Larissa said, it was better that you stayed away. Given how unexpected the win was, no one would have believed I did it on my own if you'd been there."

Zelda's voice was barely more than a whisper when she turned to face the window again. "Did my sister tell you anything else?"

"She had a lot to say. Between her and Dimitri, my head's about to explode." Dax met her gaze in the window's reflection, tapping a finger against his temple. "But she didn't say much about you. Well, except that fallout from Isadora's actions and her death was significant, and that you'd taken the brunt of the Grand Coven and Council's shit. And that you were thinking about returning to the old ways, putting some space between the coven and pack. Congratulations on the high priestess thing, by the way."

Zelda rubbed her fingers over the silver cuff on wrist, the same one Isadora had worn. "We're peas in a pod, you and me. Pushed into roles neither of us wanted."

"More like dragged kicking, punching, hollering, and bleeding in my case." Dax offered a wink as he stepped closer to her, his hand once again finding the small of her back. "At least now I have another of my twenty questions answered, Ms. Grizelda Melik—High Priestess of the Sleeping Lady Coven, and President and CEO of Mabon Enterprises. Should I bow or something?"

"Goddess, don't remind me." Zelda took a half step back, and he slid his hands around her waist. He didn't miss the contented sound of her exhale as she curled into him. "My father made it official at the emergency board meeting this morning. I'm not sure I'm up for the job. What do I know about running anything?"

"You'll do fine. From what I understand—Dimitri gave me a full press locker room pep talk before he left— leadership is all about finding the right people to delegate to. I should have called your assistant to make an appointment instead of leaving messages on your private line and showing up at Coven House or here," Dax chuckled. "So, what's your first order of business, Your Highness?"

Zelda's eyes slid shut and she took a deep breath. When she opened them again, her face was a blank mask. "Giving you this." Zelda slipped from his arms, reaching for a plain white envelope on the desk and handing it to him.

In Dax's experience, envelopes like that never contained anything good. He held his breath as he opened it and pulled out a check. "What the hell is this for?" He'd never seen so many zeroes in his life.

Zelda bowed her head, staring at the floor. "You suffered terrible things thanks to Isadora, and will suffer their consequences for the rest of your life. It's not nearly enough, but it'll get you and your family out of Anchorage, to wherever you want to go."

Anger boiled in his gut, pride speaking for him. "I don't need your charity."

"Not charity, compensation."

"With conditions, I'm guessing."

"Yeah." Zelda kept her expression and voice carefully neutral. "If you take the money, you have to leave. It's up to you if your family goes with, but I knew you wouldn't want to leave them behind, so I convinced the board to add to the original sum to cover them too."

A band tightened around his chest, and he had to force the question out. "And that's what you want? Me to leave?"

"I..." she sighed, "It doesn't matter what I want."

That she wouldn't even look at him only made his frustration surge. He caught her delicate chin between his finger and thumb, tipping it upward so she had no choice but to look at him unless she closed her eyes. Which she did, until he sighed her name. The pain behind her eyes, glittering with tears, nearly staggered him, as powerful as one of Dimitri's punches to the gut.

He released her, staring at the check. "If taking this means walking away from you..." He held the check up between them and tore it to finger-width pieces before setting them on the desk.

"You're insane."

"You're probably right. But I don't run, especially from what I want." He couldn't help but chuckle as Zelda stared at him, then the check. He could swear he saw a glimmer of relief. "Of course, I might need to if Jamie ever finds out what I just did. So, how about you? You still determined to chase me off?"

"No. I never wanted that." Zelda shook her head slowly. "I'd like to hire you."

It was Dax's turn to stare in disbelief. He couldn't have heard her correctly. "You're kidding, right?"

"It took some convincing but the board has already approved it. I just need you to sign the paperwork to make it official." She leaned past him, opening a purple folder on the desk and tapping a finger on the top page's signature line.

"But just a minute ago, you were offering me a fortune to get lost. How did you...? Why would the board...? I don't—"

"It was a gamble, I admit. My father wagered you'd take the money and run. If he lost, I won the right to offer you a job. So, what do you say?"

"And if you lost?"

"It's not important." Something about the set of Zelda's jaw told him not to push for an answer. "I was sure you'd have more integrity than that. I'm glad I was right."

"Seems I'm not the only one riding the crazy train," Dax muttered. "I already have a job, you know."

"I'm hoping you'll like my benefits package better." Thick lashes fluttered over the blue eyes peering up at him. The corners of her mouth twitched upward before turning into a grin. "Sorry. It's hard to say that and keep a straight face.

Dax returned her smile as he picked up the folder, scanning the pages within. His jaw dropped as he looked at the details. "Vice president? I'm not qualified. Hell, I don't even have a real high school diploma, just a GED. And the closest I've gotten to college was seeing a concert at the Wendy Williamson Auditorium." And screwing a co-ed in her dorm room, but Zelda didn't need to hear about that.

"It sounds more complex than it is. Your job duties are well within your skill set as I understand it, mostly focused on the pack's gym and monthly fights, not to mention handling Mabon's security when needed. Your schedule will be flexible, so you can still teach at your old gym and fulfill any duties assigned to you as beta. And it'll mesh nicely with mine. My job will require a lot of travel, stays in expensive hotels around the world. And being in charge of security, you assign my body guard. Unless you want to do it." Her cheeks pinked as she said the words.

"I don't understand. Why?"

"Why the job? Or the body guard part? I mean, isn't it obvious? Or do you object to spending the night with me in a hotel?" Her blush darkened, spreading south as her gaze dropped to his mouth, then met his eyes again. "The only thing Isadora did right was joining forces with the pack. She might not have gone about it in the best way, though. I want to fix the damage she did. And I think we work well together, complement each other."

Dax wrapped an arm around Zelda's waist and pulled her tight against him. With his other hand, he picked up a pen and scrawled his signature on the line. "What do you say we get out of here, go someplace and celebrate?"

Zelda offered a soft smile, curling her fingers in the hair at the nape of his neck and tugging him downward. Her lips brushed his as she replied, "I like the way you think, Mr. Dax Rand, Beta of Bold Peak Pack and VP of Mabon Enterprises."

CHAPTER 13

ZELDA DIDN'T KNOW HOW DAX WOULD TOP THE blindfolded drive to their destination. He'd kept her entertained through a combination of off-tune sing-alongs and wandering—in her case, blindly—hands. By the time his old Chevy pickup truck pulled to a stop, she was ready to jump him on the front bench seat.

"You ready?"

"Always." Zelda caught his hand as he unbuckled her seat belt, raising it to her mouth to nip at his fingertips.

"Try to keep it under control for a few more minutes. Then you can go wild." Dax set her hand in her lap. Zelda heard the truck door open and the vehicle shift as he slid out. "Don't move. I'll be right around to get you."

A rush of chilly air hit her right side as the passenger door opened. Zelda squealed when one hand slid behind her back and the other hooked under her knees, lifting her out of the truck. Her arms went around Dax's neck as she nuzzled into him.

"Where are you taking me?"

"Just be patient for another minute." Dax laughed, his chest rumbling against hers.

Zelda tried to focus on her other senses, but all she could smell was Dax's unique scent, and all she could hear was the crunch of his boots on fresh snow. Based on the way he moved, he was carrying her up something. Stairs, maybe. Their upward journey ended, and she heard a key turn in a lock and a door open.

Well, at least they were someplace warm. And it smelled like evergreen, cinnamon, and popcorn. The smell grew stronger as he crouched down, settling her onto something soft. He slipped off her jacket and heeled booties, kissing the top of each foot, then stretched out alongside her. His lips found hers, kissing her into breathlessness before sliding off her blindfold.

When she opened her eyes, flickering multicolor lights shined behind his head, forming a colorful halo. "What—"

He rolled onto his back, his fingers twining with hers. "Merry Christmas, Zelda. Or pre-New Years, I guess. Do you like it?"

Zelda blinked up into the lights, watching them dance along the branches. The sloped ceiling was awash with color. Her gaze swept the room, dark except for the lights on the tree. They were at Toby's house. Her eyes locked with Dax's, and she wondered if hers reflected the colorful lights as well as his did. Warmth filled her, like that moment when you get home after a long trip.

"Yes, I love it." Zelda's lips brushed his before she

climbed to her feet and stepped back from the tree, taking in the sight.

Dax stretched out on the nest of blankets and pillows, a pleased smile curling his lips as he watched her admire his work. The spruce tree rose above him at least a dozen feet, taking up nearly the entire living room. Zelda had seen carefully decorated Christmas trees around town since before Samhain, but Dax's tree was prettier than them all—packed with tiny multicolor lights, silver tinsel, and strings of popcorn and cranberries.

"My first Christmas tree. It's so pretty. And huge. When did you do this?"

"I found the tree while I was running with the pack. Last night, I cut it down and dragged it back here. I decorated it this morning before I came to your office." A wide grin lit his face. "And helpful hint—always check to see if a tree is occupied before bringing it into the house. It was like a *Looney Tunes* cartoon in here, me getting outdone by a squirrel."

"I'm sorry I missed it." Zelda laughed, enjoying the images her mind conjured of a black wolf chasing a squirrel through the house. "You must be exhausted! First all the stuff since Solstice, then fighting, now this. Have you slept at all?" *And here I was grumbling this morning about getting only six hours of sleep.*

"Dimitri says it's a side effect of the change. I seem to have plenty of energy to spare." Dax propped himself up on his elbows. "There's more gifts for you in the bathroom, hanging on the back of the door. Why don't you check them out, then meet me back out here?"

Zelda could only shake her head and offer Dax a

smile as she moved to the bathroom, flicking on the light and shutting the door behind her. Hanging there were a purple fleece tunic and flannel pants covered with penguins drinking from steaming mugs. A pair of bunny slippers sat on the floor next to empty dog dishes.

A smile split Zelda's face as she stripped out of her blouse, skirt, and stockings—somehow the shirt had lost a couple buttons between the office and Toby's house—and slipped into the cozy gifts. Some men would buy sexy lingerie, but apparently Dax had her comfort in mind. Or maybe flannel and fleece turned him on. Who was she to judge?

When she opened the door, he cried out, "Don't come out yet!"

"What are you doing?"

"Patience, angel."

She sank to the edge of the bathtub, grabbing an *Alaska* magazine to leaf through. She could hear Dax moving around—clearly trying to be quiet about it—on the other side of the door and humming Christmas carols to himself. What was he up to?

It grew quiet for a moment before Dax called to her, "Okay, you can come out now."

"I don't need to keep my eyes shut or anything?" She paused, her hand on the door knob.

When he replied with a "Nope," she left the bathroom, shuffling along the wood floor in her new slippers.

Dax sat on the pile of blankets, his legs crisscrossed and a wrapped box nestled between them. He looked like a big kid, wearing nothing but a huge grin, his tattoos, a pair of bunny slippers, and the flannel pants from their earlier stay at the cabin. A fire blazed and crackled in the wood stove, and a pair of steaming mugs and a plate of cookies sat on the floor next to him.

Dax looked down at the box in his lap. "I've got something else for you."

A laugh barked free before she could stop it. "What's in the box, Dax? Is it wrapped in a big bow?" she teased as she sank to the blankets next to him.

Dax looked confused for a second before a wolfish smile lit his face. He made a show, worthy of a stripper in a male revue, of untying the ribbon and teasing open the lid. Nestled in the tissue paper was an intricately carved wooden owl mask. Her fingers stroked the soft brown feathers along its edge.

"Do you like it?"

"It's gorgeous."

Dax stared into the box, his voice low when he spoke. "When the wolves chased me through the woods the night I died, there was a moment when I stopped running. I prayed—not something I do often—for my life. And then the owl appeared. I wanted to follow it, but I couldn't before the wolves had me. That bird—at least I'm assuming it's the same one—brought you to me so you could give me back my life. Well, maybe not *my* life, but one that I hope to make the best of. So far, it's off to an interesting start, thanks to you."

"Interesting in a good way?" Zelda was almost afraid to ask. Since meeting her, he'd been killed, turned into a werewolf, made an accessory to murder, and beat almost to death by the local pack. That dark cloud that followed her everywhere had clearly enveloped him as well. She swallowed hard as she bowed her head. "Or bad?"

He nudged her chin upward and brushed his lips against hers. His eyes crinkled at the corners as he smiled. "It's better when you're with me." He nipped teasingly at her lower lip. "Or pressed against me, squirming on top of or under me..."

"I do what I can." Zelda smiled as she shook her head, her gaze dropping to the lovely owl in the box. "I can't believe you did this all for me. But I didn't get you anything."

"Sure you did. You brought me back to life."

Zelda's heart rose in her throat, stopping her from saying anything. Instead, she carefully removed the box from Dax's lap, setting it aside as she pushed him onto his back and straddled him. She could feel the heat of him even through the fleece and flannel of her clothes as she stretched out along his length, her slippers on top of his.

His feet wiggled against hers, not to mention other parts, as he chuckled. "Gotta watch the bunnies. They're naughty little—"

She hushed him with a kiss, his lips warm and soft beneath hers. It didn't take long before the kisses turned from sweet enough to melt her heart to hot enough to melt her panties. Dax gripped the edge of her tunic and yanked it over her head. He rolled her onto her back, his mouth teasing her skin as he worked his way downward. He paused only to strip off her pants, panties, and slippers, disposing of them as quickly as her shirt.

Dax made his way back up her body, giving her sharp little bites that sent jolts of sensation through her. With all her focus on the magic his mouth and hands were working, Zelda didn't realize he'd shed his own pants until his lips found hers and he slowly pressed into her.

She freed a blissful sigh as he fully sheathed himself within her. Dax echoed the sound, his thrusts slow, almost languid.

But Zelda hungered for something else. She scraped her nails along his back until she reached the rounded muscles of his ass, then sank them in. Dax groaned against her mouth, his hips giving a rough, involuntary jerk.

"Yeah... just like that."

Dax grinned against her lips. "As you wish, High—"

Zelda shut him up with a kiss, her tongue tangling with his as he thrust into her. After a few strokes, she broke away from his mouth out of fear of biting a tongue or chipping a tooth. "Harder, Dax," she moaned past the mouthful of muscular shoulder.

He gave her exactly what she asked for, driving into her until she was gasping his name. She met him thrust for thrust, giving as good as she got, each growly breath only urging her on. As he swelled within her, she clamped her legs around his hips and pressed him deeper. He threw his head back, freeing something that sounded suspiciously like a howl, his release pushing her over the edge.

There was something satisfying about the trembling weight of him as he collapsed onto her, about the way he twitched inside her from the aftershocks. They laid tangled like that for several minutes, their breathing ragged.

"Merry Christmas," he murmured against her skin, his teeth nipping her collarbone.

Zelda seemed to have lost the ability to form words. She silently clung to Dax when he rolled onto his back, not willing to separate from him yet. Nuzzling into the crook of his neck, she rose and fell with his deep breaths.

"An interesting start." Zelda repeated Dax's earlier words, pressing her lips to the smooth skin of his chest before giving him a little bite.

His fingertips traced lightly up and down the length of her spine. "Interesting good or bad?"

"Definitely good. But you know what would make it even better?" She rolled her hips slowly against his.

"Mmm... I'm getting some ideas." His hands slid down her sides to close around her hips, pressing her down onto him as he thrust upward.

"Good to know we're of like mind." Zelda moaned as he swiveled and thrust, hitting a sweet spot within her. "Cheers to *this* being a new holiday tradition."

Dax's reply was little more than a purr. "Cheers to that, angel."

THANK YOU!

I hope you enjoyed Zelda and Dax's story. But there's more to come! I've included a sneak peek at their continuing adventures—A Heart for My Valentine. Please read on...

A HEART FOR MY VALENTINE

Midnight Sun Supernaturals Book Two

"Mmm... nothing better than morning sex," Zelda panted against Dax's neck. The cool bedsheets tangling around her were a delicious contrast to the heat of his skin.

"Almost worth enduring morning breath," Dax teased. When Zelda rewarded his quip with a smack on the ass, he grunted and bucked his hips. But he groaned appreciatively when she latched her fingernails in and swiveled her hips. "For this, I'll put up with it a bit longer."

"Just a bit?" She nipped at his collarbone.

Dax arched upward, his gaze devouring her on its way to where their bodies joined. "You feel too good for me to last much longer, angel." He glanced at the alarm clock, perched on an old trunk next to the bed. "We have a couple hours of playtime before I have to be at the warehouse for set up. Can we take it slow on the next round?"

When his brown eyes met hers, they glinted gold—a sign his inner beast was just below the surface. Every muscle in his lean body was tense as he held his breath, waiting for her answer. The wolfish grin that tugged at his lips when she nodded made her insides clench in anticipation.

Dax swooped in with a low growl, nuzzling the crook of her neck as he curled a muscular arm under her hips to pull her closer. Zelda clung to him, her legs wrapping around his waist and her arms around his chest. Everything slipped away but the sensations of his smooth chest sliding against hers, his mouth hot on her neck, the uncoiling warmth deep in her belly as he thrust into her.

Goddess, the man knows how to move.

"Uncle Dax!" a child hollered as the bedroom door flew open.

"Fuck, fuck, fuck," Dax cursed under his breath as he angled himself to hide Zelda from his niece's view while scrambling to grab a discarded blanket and pull it over them. "Hope, what did I tell you about knocking!"

"Mooommm!" Hope shrieked as she fled the room and raced down the hallway. Her feet pounded through the living room and down the stairs, making far more noise than a forty-pound kid should be capable of. "Uncle Dax and Zelda are making a baby!"

"Oh God, I'm so sorry." Dax collapsed onto Zelda, his forehead hard against her collarbone and the weight of his body almost crushing. "Again. This is getting ridiculous."

"Getting? Why didn't you lock the door?" Zelda groaned, pulling a pillow over her face.

Between their families, there were now only two people left who hadn't burst in on them midcoitus— Dax's brother-in-law Dave, who was serving with the Army in the Middle East, and his nephew Justice. But then the toddler only half-counted since Dax's sister Jennie had been holding him, asleep on her shoulder, when she'd burst in on them screwing in the shower.

Oh, how Zelda missed the absolute privacy of those blissful weeks when they'd played house in Dax's friend Toby's Eklutna cabin. She still mourned the man's return two weeks before, and not just because it severely limited their tryst locations. The cabin had been their sanctuary, a place where they could hide away from the world. Between the occupants of Coven House where she lived, the spirits drawn to her, and Dax's extended family living situation in the duplex, they had zero privacy. In the real world, there was always someone or something demanding their attention.

In response to her mournful sigh, Dax raised his head and offered a sympathetic smile. "I thought we'd be alone since Jamie's at the tournament in Fairbanks. Jennie has a key to the front door, but she never uses it."

"Apparently, your version of 'never' doesn't mean what mine does," Zelda grumbled as Dax rolled off her. She hated that moment when he withdrew, dreaded the sudden loss of his heat and emptiness at her core.

She watched a naked Dax pad across the room to grab a pair of jeans and T-shirt draped over the back of an office chair. Lean muscles flexed and rippled under his skin as he moved. Damn him for looking as good putting clothes on as taking them off. Even knowing his sister and niece could walk in on them again, all she wanted was to drag him back into bed. *Goddess give me strength...*

As he turned toward the bed, a corner of his mouth curled upward, his nostrils flaring, likely appreciating the scent of her renewed arousal. His fingertips brushed the buttons of his jeans' fly, his thumb trailing from his belly button south.

She was nearly drooling at the thought of her tongue following the same path. "Tease," Zelda grumbled. "Don't make me come over there and teach you not to toy with me."

The other corner of his mouth joined the first. "Now who's being the tease?" His grin was full of playful challenge, but before she could answer it, he shook his head roughly and buttoned his jeans. "Jennie and Hope are still here."

With a sigh, he plucked her skirt and blouse from the floor, fingering the shredded fabric. "You'll have to borrow one of my shirts. I'll deal with our visitors, and then we can make some breakfast."

He dropped the tattered remains of Zelda's clothing onto the foot of the bed and leaned in to brush his nose against hers. "Maybe we'll even be able to salvage the rest of our morning, finish what we started."

"Promise?"

"I promise to make it up to you." His kiss sealed the deal.

As he headed to the open bedroom door, Hope's singsong carried through the house, something about "special mommy-daddy hugs" and the Wile E. Coyote tattoo on Dax's "nekkid butt."

Dax stopped in the door's opening, turning back to Zelda. The touch of red on his tan cheeks surprised her. *Is he blushing?* And she thought he had no shame, wasn't easily embarrassed. Her own cheeks were still blazing hot enough to set the pillows on fire.

"You know..." Dax stared down at his toes as he curled them into the carpet at the threshold. "You could keep some things here. I cleared out a drawer for you, and it's just been sitting empty for weeks."

Zelda's gaze darted to the tall oak dresser. Just a simple piece of furniture, but the way her mouth went dry and her heart pounded, its drawers should have been brimming with demons. She opened her mouth to respond, but nothing came out.

Her gaze swung toward Dax, finding him watching her under cover of dark lashes. When Zelda only offered a weak nod, the muscle along his jaw clenched. *Shit.* That meant he was struggling not to say anything more. And that muscle had been getting quite the workout lately. Freeing an exasperated breath, he turned and walked out of the bedroom.

The last thing Zelda wanted was to argue with Dax, especially when he'd done nothing wrong. If anything, he was doing everything right. The man was damn near perfect—thoughtful, patient, generous, responsive, funny, playful, hot as hell, a fabulous lover...

It would be so easy to go back to playing house with him, as long as she avoided eating anything he cooked or drinking any coffee he brewed. But she didn't belong in his family's duplex any more than he belonged at Coven House. Talking about their living arrangements, about the future of their relationship, always seemed to end in arguments and hurt feelings.

His acceptance of their intense connection was as frustrating to her as her resistance was to him. Why couldn't he understand that it was better to keep some distance between them? Their domestic bliss at the Eklutna cabin had shown her that much. It had been too easy, comfortable, like they'd been together forever.

But they'd only known each other since Solstice, just shy of eight weeks. Instant connection, love at first sight, didn't happen in real life. It was the binding magic. It had to be.

Unless she wanted to believe the werewolves, with their nonsense about fated mates. But then it was hard to deny when faced with Larissa and Dimitri's happiness. Zelda's sister and her alpha mate were as unlikely a pair as she'd ever seen—the sweet witch with the brutish werewolf—but their bond seemed unbreakable. It was more likely that Dimitri's bite and his presence during Larissa's First Turn was what really bound them together —the werewolf curse and imprinting doing their thing.

But what if the werewolves were on to something? Zelda rolled to wrap herself around Dax's pillow, absorbing his lingering heat and breathing in his scent. If she was stronger, she'd... what? End their relationship before they got too attached? Hot tears burned her eyes as she curled tighter into the pillow.

She tried not to listen to the angry voices echoing through the duplex. Even with the pillow over her head, she could hear them—Jennie taking issue with Zelda's "sinful ways" and Dax defending her. His lower rumble was harder to make out, but she heard words like "sweet," "trustworthy," and "kindhearted" as he sang her praises to a woman who wasn't likely to ever believe them. Zelda wrapped the blanket around herself like a shield, climbing out of the bed to shut the bedroom door the rest of the way.

Great. Now I'm ruining Dax's relationship with his family.

Eventually, Dax would calm Jennie down and convince her to leave. Zelda just needed to hide out in his bedroom, out of the line of fire, until it was safe. But the doorbell, followed by Jennie yelling for her, foiled Zelda's plans.

Who would come here looking for me? One of her coven sisters, maybe? They were the only ones who knew she was there.

"I'll be right down." Her response was higher pitched than normal, sounding more like a timid, ashamed girl than an independent, powerful witch. Damn the woman for making her feel that way.

Zelda's eyes swept the room, looking for her bra and panties. Scraps of red silk and lace dotted the gray carpet next to the bed like scattered rose petals, a reminder of the night before.

Their evening had started as a purely professional one. Zelda and Dax, in their new roles as President and Vice President of Mabon Enterprises, had met with Hiro and Suiko Hayashi, longtime clients of the company. The couple were making a brief stop in Anchorage while on their whirlwind trip to see the northern lights. Dax had thoroughly charmed the kitsune pair over dinner with stories of running the forests under the aurora, not to mention places to privately watch them. They were so impressed that they not only agreed to enlist Mabon in setting up northern lights excursion packages for visiting Japanese supernaturals but also to help sponsor future fights.

They hadn't been the only ones charmed by the werewolf. Even the innocent brush of Dax's knee against hers was enough to send her heart fluttering and instigate increasingly flirtatious but covert touches under cover of the white linen tablecloth. By the time dinner had ended and they were back in semiprivacy of Zelda's car, all bets were off. Dax—likely drawing heavily on his supernatural reflexes—somehow managed to avoid crashing as her hands and mouth explored him. He even managed to cut the twenty-minute drive between the restaurant and his house in half. It had been a good thing, since they'd barely made it as far as the bedroom before completely surrendering to their need. Her clothes had paid the price for their restraint, especially her flimsy undergarments.

Rather than go commando in what remained of her skirt, she grabbed a pair of Dax's sweatpants and T-shirt from the dresser. Her reflection in the mirror on the back of the bedroom door told her how ridiculous the ill-fitting clothes and bed hair looked. She dragged hasty fingers through the long blonde strands, twisting them into a messy bun as she left the bedroom.

The carpet was plush beneath her bare feet as she headed through the living room and down the stairs to the duplex's entry. She could see a uniformed man through the leaded glass panel on the front door. *A courier? Why would someone send a delivery to me at Dax's house instead of Coven House or Mabon's office?*

The courier shot her an impatient frown as she opened the door. "Grizelda Melik?" When Zelda nodded, he asked, "Got ID?"

Shit! Where did I drop my purse last night? "I... I do. But, umm... I'll need a minute to find it."

The courier's gaze swept over her, stuttering over her nipples where they jutted against the light cotton of the oversized anime T-shirt. His leer told her he knew she wasn't wearing her own clothes, or a bra. *Nothing like doing the dance of shame for a complete stranger.* And since Jennie had answered the door, she could only imagine what he was thinking. Her cheeks burned hot. Again.

"Just... umm... give me a minute." She took a step back from the door, starting to shut it.

A frown furrowed his brow as he stuck out a booted foot to stop the door from closing, then peered at his watch. "No time. I've got twenty other deliveries to make before noon." He shoved a clipboard toward her with one hand, while holding the small box in the other.

"Who's it from?" Zelda peered at the clipboard as she hastily scrawled her name.

"Beats me." He shrugged as he retrieved the clipboard from Zelda and handed her the box. "Guess you'll find out when you open it. Enjoy the rest of your morning," he said with a wink.

Zelda watched for a moment as the man carefully

trotted along the icy sidewalk to his waiting van. When she turned back into the house, Dax was standing on the stairs leading down to the den.

"Flaming hells," Zelda gasped, her hand flying up to muffle her thumping heart, "how long have you been standing there?"

Dax's nostrils flared, his gaze locking on the box in her hands. Mahogany eyes glinted gold, a low growl vibrating the air. "Zelda, give me that box."

ABOUT THE AUTHOR

Adventure; romance; spunky, kick-ass heroines; hunky, take-charge heroes; a dash of humor... Elizabeth Allyn-Dean writes paranormal romance, urban fantasy, and fantasy stories that blends these elements to get to a happily ever after. From the first time she cracked open a fantasy novel in the treehouse she built herself, Elizabeth knew she wanted to be an author. After a detour into the world of archaeology, she shifted to editing and writing. Elizabeth loves reading, exploring her creative side, gardening, beach-combing for interesting treasures, indulging her inner geek, and playing with her two dogs and cat. For the last twenty years, she has called Alaska home, enjoying the adventures, gorgeous scenery, and fascinating people and places it offers.